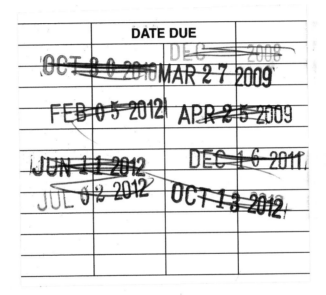

Marley Z

and the

Bloodstained Violin

Marley Z

and the

Bloodstained Violin

JIM FUSILLI

DUTTON CHILDREN'S BOOKS

DUTTON CHILDREN'S BOOKS

A division of Penguin Young Readers Group

PUBLISHED BY THE PENGUIN GROUP

Penguin Group (USA) Inc., 375 Hudson Street, New York, New York 10014, U.S.A. | Penguin Group (Canada), 90 Eglinton Avenue East, Suite 700, Toronto, Ontario, Canada M4P 2Y3 (a division of Pearson Penguin Canada Inc.) | Penguin Books Ltd, 80 Strand, London WC2R 0RL, England | Penguin Ireland, 25 St Stephen's Green, Dublin 2, Ireland (a division of Penguin Books Ltd) | Penguin Group (Australia), 250 Camberwell Road, Camberwell, Victoria 3124, Australia (a division of Pearson Australia Group Pty Ltd) | Penguin Books India Pvt Ltd, 11 Community Centre, Panchsheel Park, New Delhi - 110 017, India | Penguin Group (NZ), 67 Apollo Drive, Rosedale, North Shore 0632, New Zealand (a division of Pearson New Zealand Ltd) | Penguin Books (South Africa) (Pty) Ltd, 24 Sturdee Avenue, Rosebank, Johannesburg 2196, South Africa | Penguin Books Ltd, Registered Offices: 80 Strand, London WC2R 0RL, England

Library of Congress Cataloging-in-Publication Data

Fusilli, Jim.

Marley Z and the bloodstained violin / Jim Fusilli. — 1st ed.

p. cm.

Summary: Fourteen-year-old Marley Zimmerman is convinced that her friend did not steal a valuable violin from the Julliard School, despite surveillance video evidence, and enlists the other members of her would-be band, the Kingston Cowboys, to help her find the truth.

ISBN: 978-0-525-47907-9

[1. Stealing—Fiction. 2. Violin—Fiction. 3. Schools—Fiction. 4. Bands (Music)—Fiction. 5. New York (N.Y.)—Fiction. 6. Mystery and detective stories.] I. Title.

PZ7.F96668Mar 2008 [Fic]—dc22 2007028288

Published in the United States by Dutton Children's Books, a division of Penguin Young Readers Group

345 Hudson Street, New York, New York 10014

www.penguin.com/youngreaders

Designed by Heather Wood

Printed in the USA

First Edition

1 3 5 7 9 10 8 6 4 2

Dedicated to
the Coolest People in the World:

Readers!

Marley Z
and the
Bloodstained Violin

chapter 1

Marley Z was a diligent student, but her algebra teacher made diligence almost impossible. Mr. Noonan, who looked like a hedgehog in old corduroy, always spoke in a slow dull monotone that concealed how he felt about the day's lesson. Today, only the unexpected arrival of several police cars outside the school building provided Marley with a distraction from his lack of enthusiasm.

"He's the most boringest teacher on the planet," she told her father last week. "Maybe the most boringest person ever."

"You've been at the Beacon School for, what, three days?" He set two wheaty placemats on the kitchen island, meaning Marley's mother would be late again. "Three days and you know this?"

The summer study program and last month's orientation had given her a veteran sense of comfort.

"If there's somebody more boring, I'd like to meet him," she replied.

Zeke Zimmerman drew up, soup bowls in his hands. "Really?" he asked, eyebrow raised, as if Marley actually meant what she said.

Marley turned to her baby sister; oblivious to the conversation, Skeeter rattled a colorful set of plastic rings on her high-chair tray. "And he smells like mothballs," Marley told her, "and he has tufts of gray hair in his ears."

Thinking his daughter was talking about him, not the boring Mr. Noonan, Marley's father put the bowls on the tile-topped island. Frowning, he lifted his old bleached-gray denim shirt to smell his lanky frame, then ran a finger along his outer ear.

"Not you, Dad," Marley sighed. "Mr. Noonan."

Skeeter cooed happily.

A pot of gumbo burbled on the stove, and the pleasing scent of thyme and dark roux filled the brownstone. Marley had brought home crabmeat and catfish fillets from Citarella's on Broadway and 75th. Having eaten her father's cooking for four-teen years, Marley knew he had a lot more energy than skill as a chef, but fresh ingredients sometimes made a difference.

Her father said cooking turned a house into a home. Even if her mother only ate dinner with them on the weekends. Most weekends.

Seated in the last row by the classroom's sun-streaked windows, Marley was awakened from her half-daydream, half-memory trip by the appearance of Vice Principal Otto at the door.

Mr. Noonan put down his chalk and ambled hedgehog-like across the room, all the while continuing the lesson.

"The reservoir in Central Park is one hundred and six acres in diameter," he droned, "and rain is falling at a rate of a quarter-inch per hour. To write an expression for the amount of water, in gallons, in the reservoir after m hours . . ."

Sixteen sets of eyes followed him. Marley watched as Mr. Noonan stepped into the corridor. White clouds appeared as he dusted his hands together.

He listened attentively to Miss Otto, who was as forceful as he was not, and returned a few seconds later.

"Marisol," he said. "Come here, please."

As tiny Marisol Poveda slid from her desk chair in the front row, Vice Principal Otto jutted her head into the classroom.

"Marley," she said, beckoning with her fingers. "You'd better come along too."

Marley Z gathered her things, dropping her calculator into the pouch of her carpenter's jeans. She slipped her pencil behind her ear, much as her dad would do when she'd stop by his studio for advice or to retrieve Skeeter for their afternoon playdate.

𝔪iss Otto introduced the man in her office as Detective Sergeant Sampson. Broad-shouldered and brawny in a gray suit, striped tie and a pale-blue shirt, Sgt. Sampson towered over Miss Otto and Marisol, who was the smallest girl in Beacon's freshman class. Marley was tall, soon to be six feet, as both of her parents were, and her sprouting dreadlocks added to her height. But Sgt. Sampson seemed to tower over her too, filling Miss Otto's office, which sat above the school's main entrance on West 61st Street.

"Girls," Miss Otto said, pointing to the chairs in front of her desk as she shut the door. A uniformed police officer stood outside, ready to block anyone from entering.

Marisol sat, and Marley did too. They looked at each other. Marisol was usually as carefree as a butterfly. But now Marley saw concern in her friend's dark eyes.

Sgt. Sampson placed an elbow on the khaki-green filing cabinets, brushing aside the leaves of a spider plant.

"Do you know why you're here, Miss Poveda?" he asked, his face as taut as a clenched fist.

Marisol shook her head. Her black hair shimmered under the overhead lights.

"Where is it?" he asked.

"I'm sorry. I don't—"

"The violin," the policeman said. "Where is it?"

"My violin?" Marisol replied. "It's in my room at home. Why—?"

"Miss Otto," Sgt. Sampson said, nodding toward a TV on the rolling cart.

Standing at the side of her desk, the vice principal reached to press a button on the VCR.

A wave of static on the monitor disappeared and a soundless black-and-white video began to play.

Marley thought she recognized the vast space on the screen. It was somewhere in the Juilliard School, which was only a short walk away at Lincoln Center on 65th Street.

In the center of the fuzzy video was a black base topped by a Lucite cube, the kind that usually held a small sculpture or a bust. Inside the display cube was a violin. The camera angle made it difficult to see its details.

Marley frowned. The policeman's sharp, accusing tone as he mentioned a missing violin; and now a video of a violin on display at the best music conservatory in the nation: No, she thought. This is not good.

On screen, a security guard paced past the cube, his arms folded behind his back.

Sgt. Sampson said, "Miss Poveda . . ."

Marisol looked up at the policeman.

"It's better that you tell me now."

She raised her hands from the thighs of her black jeans. "I don't . . . I don't understand," she said nervously, her native Ecuador in her accent. She turned to the vice principal. "Miss Otto . . ."

On the tape, the security guard continued to pace. Then he stopped, turned and, alarmed, suddenly bolted out of the frame, as if to check on an emergency in another part of the lobby.

Now the instrument, cube and base stood unguarded.

And smoke began to billow from a corner of the room.

As Marley watched, Marisol appeared on the monitor and hurried toward the instrument.

The brown-skinned girl wore a white peasant blouse with puff sleeves, jeans, and huarache sandals that matched her belt. Marley had seen her friend many times in those clothes. Bought at the little Latin American boutique on Columbus Avenue where Marisol's mother worked, the delicate blouse had red threads woven into the sleeves and scoop neckline.

As the smoke cloud in the Juilliard lobby drew nearer, Marisol stopped, raised on her toes, lifted the cube and tossed it to the carpet.

Marley thought, *Why wasn't the cube bolted down?*

Then Marisol snatched the instrument by the neck, tucked it under her arm, and, strings against her ribs and belt, dashed out of the frame.

The policeman gestured, and Miss Otto turned off the monitor.

"Miss Poveda?" he said.

"I—I did not do that," she replied, as tears welled.

Sgt. Sampson shook his head tiredly as he stepped from the filing cabinet to stand above Marisol. "Miss Poveda, we just saw—"

"I did not do it. I wouldn't. I would not steal."

Marisol trembled in the chair. Marley reached for her hand.

"Where is it?" Sgt. Sampson demanded.

"I don't—I don't know," she cried. "I am not a thief!"

Sgt. Sampson turned and wrapped a knuckle against Miss

Otto's door. The policewoman who had been standing guard opened it and peered in.

"Take her down to the precinct," the sergeant said, jabbing a finger toward Marisol.

"No!" Marisol shouted.

"Sergeant," Miss Otto said, "please . . ."

"Tell her parents they can pick her up at the Two-Oh. But not before she returns that violin."

Marisol was terrified. "Miss Otto, my mother is working, and my father—"

"Marisol, please tell them where you took that instrument," the vice principal said.

"But I didn't—I didn't take it."

As the policewoman reached for her elbow, Marisol shook and sobbed. Marley lifted a tissue from the box on Miss Otto's desk and passed it to her distraught friend.

"Marisol," Marley whispered gently, in an attempt to comfort her.

Another uniformed police officer came to the office door. "Detective," he said, "it's not in her locker."

Turning to Marisol, Sgt. Sampson said, "You can save yourself and your family, Miss Poveda. Tell me where you hid the violin."

Miss Otto said, "Sergeant, please."

"Miss Otto, do you have any idea how much that violin is worth?"

Before she could reply, he said, "It's valued in excess of five hundred thousand dollars."

Marisol gasped.

Sgt. Sampson said, "A half-million—"

"Yes, we know, Sergeant." Miss Otto had a reputation for a fiery temper and was known to stand firm with her students. "Let me talk to her. Will ten minutes make a difference?"

"Yes," he said sharply, "it might."

As Marley watched, Sgt. Sampson looked down at Marisol and said, "Miss Poveda, you are under arrest for grand larceny. Which is a felony. Which means you are going to jail."

"Sergeant!" Miss Otto protested.

Tears had spilled onto Marisol's blouse.

"Jackson," Sampson barked to the policewoman. "Get her out of here."

"Marley . . ." Marisol reached desperately for her friend, but the policewoman stepped between them. And then she led Marisol out of the office.

Sgt. Sampson followed.

Short, plump Miss Otto folded her arms across the front of her suit. "The pictures are real," she said plainly.

Marley nodded. "No doubt. But . . ."

The vice principal's mind raced. Sgt. Sampson had requested the school's security tapes, and said the NYPD would search every locker in the building to find the missing violin. She knew the chaos would disrupt the entire school.

Suddenly, Marley said, "She didn't do it. Not like that."

"Marley . . ."

"I know she didn't."

"You know it?"

"Absolutely. You know too," she said.

Miss Otto unfolded her arms and placed her palms on her desk. With fifteen years experience in high school administration, Vivianna Otto wasn't naive. Young students had deceived her, especially early in her career. But she had come to believe that she had an instinct for recognizing the good in every young person, and she found nothing more satisfying than helping a student she believed in, especially when few others did.

With someone like Marley, it was easy. Marley's mother was the most influential African-American lawyer on Wall Street, her father a renowned comic-book writer and illustrator and, as she learned during the summer, Marley was bright and curious, outgoing and superconfident. Turned out everyone on the Upper West Side seemed to know the fourteen-year-old with coffee-light skin, cascading dreadlocks, eccentric clothes and natural bounce in her step. Even Miss Otto's energetic father, who ran an Italian restaurant on 70th Street, admired her.

But Marisol was a different case. Though outwardly friendly and cheerful, she bore the weight of her family's hopes and aspirations on her little shoulders. The Poveda family had come north to New York City so their children could live the American dream. For Marisol, a talented musician, it meant attending the Beacon School, studying the violin with private tutors and, four years from now, gaining acceptance into Juilliard. A career in an internationally acclaimed orchestra or as a tutor herself could follow.

Marley said, "Would Marisol risk everything—her reputation, her future, her *freedom*—to steal an instrument guarded by uniformed officers and a video security system? At Juilliard?"

No, Miss Otto thought. Nor were there any signs in Marisol's behavior to suggest she was a lowly thief.

"Marley," she said, "I think I do know it. I don't believe Marisol would steal. But we saw the violin in her hands—"

"Yes, but she insists she didn't do it. Even though we saw that she did."

Miss Otto went to her desk drawer. "I'm going to have to call her parents," she said. "And they're going to have to get a lawyer."

Marley asked, "Can I have a copy of that tape?" The Film department had the kind of equipment that could duplicate the video onto a disk in no time.

Miss Otto said, "Marley, that security tape proves she took—"

"Yes, but there's got to be something there," Marley said. "Something that proves what we saw isn't the whole story. That what Marisol said is true."

Marley wriggled sideways past the vice principal to press a button on the VCR. With a mechanical whir, the tape cassette appeared. Marley snatched it and slid it into the pocket of her carpenter's jeans.

"I'll do my best," she said, superconfidently.

chapter 2

THREE WEEKS EARLIER

The members of the Kingston Cowboys first came together during the best week of the year in New York, that wondrous period in August right before Labor Day when many natives flee for one last nip of vacation and the city seems to pause ever so slightly to take a deep breath.

On this mellow afternoon, from a perch on the long, crowded steps of the Metropolitan Museum of Art, Marley Zimmerman and her best friend Teddy So were happy to watch the tourists soak up the city's endless beauty—not just the Museum Mile that stretched along tree-lined Fifth Avenue, but also the parks, the amazing architecture, the monuments, restaurants and shops; the musicals on Broadway, rock shows downtown or jazz in the Greenwich Village clubs; and the sights at Rockefeller Center, Soho, the Lower East Side, the Upper West Side, Chinatown, Wall Street and Harlem.

While Teddy bounded on stubby legs toward an ice-cream truck, Marley noted how the remaining New Yorkers had slowed down too so they also could savor all the beauty that surrounded them, sipping the city's pleasures rather than gulping them down as usual. Chin balanced on fists, elbows on her knees, Marley smiled at the thought that today even the taxicabs on the half-empty streets just seemed to glide along.

So far, it had been a great week. Echoing the easy pace surrounding her, Marley set out to explore the city. On Monday morning, she went to Bryant Park behind the 42nd Street library and lazed in the grass while Skeeter skittered and stumbled chasing pigeons and squirrels. Then she took her down to the southern tip of the island to watch the sailboats on the Hudson, sharing a gyro sandwich she bought from a singing street vendor. Yesterday, while Skeeter stayed in their dad's studio, she and Teddy rode the 2 train over to Brooklyn for the scents and sights of the Botanical Garden, then switched to the Q train in Park Slope to ride way out to Coney Island for a hot dog at Nathan's and a scary trip on the rickety Cyclone rollercoaster.

Everywhere she went she took her sweet time, doing what she wanted to.

This morning, she decided to walk with Teddy across the Great Lawn in Central Park and hang around the Met while they waited for Marisol, who promised a surprise. Now, amid a gazillion tourists on the museum steps, she and Teddy shared an orange Popsicle as they talked to a boy they'd met not fifteen minutes ago.

"We're doing nothing," Marley had said, shading her eyes. "Join us."

It seemed unlikely that the boy would. Of all the people on the Met's steps and down on the sunny avenue, he was the only person wearing a suit. A black one, perfectly tailored. And a bow tie.

But he did. With a formality Marley assumed was his habit, he introduced himself as Bassekou Sissoko. From Mali.

He started to stick out his hand, but seeing Marley's and Teddy's fingers were coated with sticky orangey sugar, he nodded instead.

"Where is the famous chaos of New York City?" he asked.

"On vacation," Marley replied, squinting. "Are you going to sit? Looking up at you is burning my retinas."

Bassekou came down the steps until his shadow covered Marley.

"Where do you go to school?" Teddy asked.

"I will be attending Collegiate."

"Teddy too," Marley said.

"I didn't see you at orientation," Teddy said.

Bassekou shrugged. "My father insisted I have my own orientation. He's the ambassador to the United Nations from my country. I don't think he will agree to permit me to become an ordinary American boy."

Earlier, Marley had kicked off her flip-flops. Now she rolled up the bottom of her tatty jeans to expose her tanned legs to the sun's soothing rays. Teddy's pudgy legs were already catching the sun: He wore shiny green basketball shorts that draped below his knees.

"He has sent me here to study the American collection," Bassekou continued, nodding toward the museum's entrance.

"If you want chaos, you'll find it in there," Marley said, throwing her thumb over her shoulder. "Not many New Yorkers, though . . . Not this week."

"But you are New Yorkers," Bassekou said. "Weren't you born here?"

"You don't have to be born in New York City to be a native New Yorker," Marley said. "You just have to be someone who's been living here for a while."

"New York City will take you in. You'll see," added Teddy, the only member of his family to be born outside of Taiwan. "It happens all the time."

"Your father . . . ?" Bassekou led.

"Runs an import business in Chinatown. Marley's dad is 3Z."

Bassekou failed to understand.

"The Time Traveler? The comics, the books . . . ? Mr. Zimmerman writes and draws them. He's writing the movie too."

"Ah," said Bassekou. Clearly, he'd never heard of her father or the series.

Marley was relieved. She'd been fending off false friendships from teenage boys for years—all of them, it seemed, wanted to be either 3Z or, worse, Mike Barnett, Time Traveler.

Though none of the boys who turned up on the steep steps of their brownstone had been from Mali . . .

"I must learn more about your father," Bassekou said.

Marley turned to find Marisol and a lanky boy in a Collegiate T-shirt, well-pressed jeans and new sneakers climbing the Met's steps.

She rose to greet her friend. As had become their custom, they kissed each other on both cheeks.

Teddy grimaced.

"What have you been doing?" Marisol asked.

"Talking to Bassekou. You?"

She said, "I found us a drummer. He's Wendell. He just moved here from Jersey."

"You go to Collegiate too?" Teddy asked.

The boy's cheeks flushed red, and his Adam's apple bobbed as he swallowed. Finally, he managed to say, "Next week."

"Me too," Teddy told him. "And Bassekou."

"See?" Marisol said to Wendell. "Now you know somebody at your new school."

"Two," Marley added, holding up two fingers.

Thinking she had flashed him the '60s peace sign, Wendell Justice held up two fingers too. Then he about died of embarrassment: Even with her shoes off, her frayed jeans rolled up to her knees and her lips a bright orange, Marley was the most fantastic person he'd ever seen. And now he'd come across like a total dweeb.

"Wendell's grandfather was a carnival barker," Marisol said quickly.

For a moment, that unexpected bit of news seemed to make everything all right.

~

Marley hurried back from the film lab and gave the Juilliard security tape to Mr. Lawson, the office secretary. Before returning to her classes—Mr. Noonan's drone-a-thon was over by now—she peered into Miss Otto's room. She was behind her desk, talking on her phone and jotting down notes while Sgt. Sampson squawked into his cell.

Marley rushed away from the tension and toward her locker. Her geography class was already underway. As she hurried along, her dreadlocks flopping, she wondered how she would concentrate on the afternoon's lessons.

Four hours later, Marley, her father, baby Skeeter and Teddy watched the copy of the video on the little TV/DVD they kept on the kitchen island. Sharing pigeon peas and rice, and a cucumber-and-lime salad, they stared intently at the screen, Marley seated on a stool next to Skeeter's high chair, Zeke Z standing across from her, his back to the stove in case anyone wanted seconds.

Teddy didn't know whether to sit or stand.

"Okay, what do you guys see?" Marley said, pointing with her fork.

"Even though she's rushing, Marisol looks like a zombie," her father replied.

"Exactly," Marley said. "Does she usually look like that?"

"No," Teddy said. "She's got kind of a happy expression."

"Good. That's one."

Skeeter made a funny sour face as she chomped a slice of lime-seasoned cucumber.

"What else?" Marley asked.

Zeke Z shook his head and shrugged.

Marley rewound the video; on screen, Marisol backed toward the empty display, and the smoke seemed to recede. "Look how she grabs the violin."

"By the neck," Teddy said.

"By the *neck*. Marisol knows how to handle a violin. You don't just snatch it up by the neck. Especially one that's so valuable it's in a display case with security cameras and stuff."

Next, they saw Marisol tuck the instrument against her hip.

"That looks like a good way to ruin the strings," said Zeke Z, his mouth full of pigeon peas.

"Bang! Marisol carries her violin every day. *Every day.* She knows you can't go around wrecking the strings by letting them drag against your belt."

Teddy said, "At band practice, she carries her violin like Marley carries Skeeter."

"Her parents saved for it," Marley added. "A lot."

Deep, soulful jazz floated from Zeke Z's office upstairs. The Zimmerman brownstone was more than 125 years old. They'd restored it, and it was beautiful, but sound leaked through the walls and wooden floors. Marley heard everything: her dad's snores, Skeeter's midnight baby cries and their mother coming in late and leaving early.

"Speaking of security, Marley," her father said. "Why wasn't the display bolted down tight? And what about an alarm?"

"I thought about that," she replied. "The fire alarm probably went off at the same time as the alarm on the display case. As for the thing not being bolted down . . . well, don't you think that proves somebody else is involved?"

"You're right," Teddy said. "Marisol doesn't have a screwdriver or anything with her. That cube was already loose."

"See those faint little tracks on the carpet?" Marley said, pointing at the screen. "They probably move the display case to a storage area at night. I'll bet that's when somebody opened it."

"Still," Marley's father said, "she's got the violin. That's pretty persuasive evidence."

"But not as persuasive as before Marley became involved," Teddy replied. He nodded enthusiastically.

Zeke Z studied his daughter as she stared at the screen for additional clues. Had his friend been arrested for larceny, he would've been terribly upset. But Marley had her mother's resolve. When something was wrong, mother and daughter focused on the problem and set out to make things right. It was a very admirable trait.

"We'll have to prove Marisol didn't do it," Marley said. "At least not like the police think she did." As she stood, she added, "First, I'm going to talk to her parents. They should know what we've found out."

Teddy grabbed his napkin and wiped his lips. "I'm coming."

Skeeter let out a gleeful squeal as if she was delighted that dinner was over. A mound of rice and peas had gathered on the floor beneath her seat.

"Be safe," Zeke Z muttered as the two teens fled.

Seconds later, Teddy returned to the Zimmerman's kitchen.

"I'm helping you with the dishes," he said, a bit dejected.

chapter 3

The Kingston Cowboys were still on the steps when Bassekou emerged from his tour of the Met.

Actually, they were back on the steps, having returned from introducing Wendell to the Central Park Zoo and the Carousel—Marley smiled at the memory of Teddy and Marisol bobbing up and down on the 100-year-old hand-carved horses, sweet calliope music surrounding them. They also told him about the coffee shop on 69th and Broadway where they gathered after class. Now that Teddy would be attending a different school than Marley and Marisol, they'd pinkie-pledged to continue to meet there, no matter what.

"It is more or less equidistant between Collegiate and Beacon," Teddy offered thoughtfully.

Marisol said, "It's now our official band hangout, Wendell."

Marley noticed Wendell looked down and blushed whenever anyone addressed him. Earlier, when they exchanged cell phone numbers, his cheeks turned candy-apple red. She wondered how he got up the nerve to answer the "drummer wanted" ad Marisol placed on the Web's Gigfinder and Bandmix boards.

"The Kingston Cowboys," Bassekou repeated when Marisol told him the group's new name. "And what kind of music do you play?"

"It's a kind of blend of reggae and country," Teddy said, gesturing with stout hands. "With some pop and rock in there too. Completely unique."

"How does it sound?" he asked, wondering if his instrument could fit their mix.

"Well . . . ," Teddy hesitated.

"We haven't practiced yet," Marley replied.

The five teens had begun to walk down the jam-packed steps.

"So," Bassekou said, "as of right now, you are the most wonderful group in the world."

"Yeah," Marley said, "exactly."

Next to the Met, a long line of vendors and artists stretched south all the way to the 79th Street transverse through Central Park. Under shady trees, paintings, sculptures, photos, jewelry and all sorts of arts and crafts were sold from flimsy card tables and carefully constructed booths that could be taken apart at the end of each day.

Among the artists and political activists with their posters and petitions was a palm reader and, at the far end, Mahjoob, who sold talismans he claimed had mystical powers.

Marley knew Mahjoob's talismans—which he said were magical stones from ancient Mesopotamia that for centuries had granted their owners long life and success—were actually rocks he'd dug up in the park. Most of the tourists figured as much: In his white robe and sparkly turban, Mahjoob was entertaining, and they thought the purchase of a New York City rock was a small price to pay for his show. Marley's dad wasn't so sure. "That guy's what they call a confidence man," he'd said. "He wins your confidence and takes advantage of your trust. Then he rips you off."

"He *is* fascinating," Bassekou said thoughtfully.

Sensing his interest, Mahjoob beckoned the boy from Mali. But, nodding politely, Bassekou continued with Marley along the path.

Also at the street fair today was a grubby musician in a tattered brown suit, ratty beige vest and a shirt that had turned a soiled gray. The tall, angular man, who *really* needed a shave, played the violin as if he wanted to shred its strings.

Marley and Bassekou stopped to hear him, but Marisol kept walking, Teddy scurrying to keep pace with her. Confused, Wendell didn't know where to go, but he decided to join Marisol, who was his first friend in his new neighborhood.

At the curb, two policemen on horseback watched as the violinist known as Tabakovic continued his violent performance for a small group that had gathered in the sun.

He finished with a dramatic flurry of notes. When the crowd began to applaud, he angrily pointed his bow toward his open violin case, which held scattered coins and a few dollar bills.

"Notice anything?" Marley said, as she and Bassekou resumed their walk.

"The man hates Tchaikovsky," Bassekou replied. "I have never heard the finale of the *Concerto in D Major* played with such aggression."

"Did you see his shoes?" Marley asked. "They're pretty new, and expensive. That whole poor-musician thing? It's kind of an act."

"Is it necessary? I wouldn't think so. . . ."

When they caught up to the group, Marley said, "Bassekou wants to know if Tabakovic has to do that."

"No," Marisol snapped. "He's talented. Very talented. That's why I refuse to listen. It's awful what he does."

Bassekou said, "I'm sorry, but I do not—"

Teddy said, "He probably makes more money than a lot of serious musicians. He does that crazy act all over the Upper West Side too."

Wendell observed the conversation, his head swiveling as if he were watching a tennis match.

Marisol said, "Late at night, he is in Damrosch Park—you know, behind Lincoln Center—and he plays beautifully. Very tender and gentle. Saint-Saëns, Massenet . . . My father took me to hear. He wastes his gifts with this very ugly routine."

Teddy said, "I heard he went to Juilliard. A long time ago. They kicked him out."

Marley decided to change the subject. "If you want to check out more old American art, the Frick Collection is up the block. They've got lots of cool stuff by Whistler. . . ."

~

ᗰarley felt bad about leaving Teddy behind with her father, Skeeter and the dirty dishes—he was a sensitive boy—but she believed she would find heartache at Marisol's apartment. She hoped the Povedas would let *her* in.

With the sun about to dip behind the Jersey Palisades, a little bit of a chill was in the air. Heading west to Broadway for the trip uptown, Marley regretted she hadn't put on a hoodie.

"Hey."

She heard a boy's voice behind her, but she didn't stop.

"Marley. Wait."

When she reached the bright lights of funky Columbus Avenue, she turned.

It was Ben Rosenberg.

Marley groaned. Ben was one of the 3Z scruffs who would hang around her brownstone to catch a glimpse of her father.

He trotted to catch up. "Hey, Marley." His T-shirt announced that he watched the Discovery Channel. "Heard you stopped by the film lab today."

Ben had a manila envelope in his hand.

"Look," she replied, "I'm kind of in a rush—"

He opened the envelope. Fearing it was a comic Ben wanted her father to autograph, Marley cringed.

But it was a smaller envelope, a square only slightly bigger than the size of a DVD.

"Next time, tell them to start at the very beginning," Ben said.

Marley realized Ben was right. She'd asked the girls in the lab to copy only the section of the security video Sgt. Sampson had shown.

As she accepted the envelope and DVD, she said, "Have you watched this?"

"I heard you said not to. . . ."

"But . . . ?"

"We're with you, Marley," he said. "Okay?"

She thanked him. "I owe you, Ben."

"Just tell the Time Traveler I said hi."

Marley chuckled as she waved good-bye.

$\mathcal{T}$en minutes later, she entered a small, third-floor walk-up filled with sorrow and worry.

Marisol and her parents had been sitting around the kitchen table. Cristina Poveda has been crying. Marisol too. Her eyes were ringed in red.

Marley figured Gus Poveda, who was the midnight-to-noon super at a luxury building on West End Avenue, had been pacing while the family held its conference.

"She didn't do it," Marley said, even before Mr. Poveda had closed the door behind her.

Mrs. Poveda talked quickly to her husband in Spanish—he spoke very little English—and then came around the round table to take Marley's hand.

"We believe her," Mrs. Poveda said. "But the police . . ."

"They were here," Marisol told her friend. "They searched the apartment."

"They looked where my husband works," Mrs. Poveda added. "The shop where I work too."

"We're going to lose everything," Marisol said, a choke in her voice. Marley looked past the old refrigerator. At the end of the narrow corridor, peering through a glass-beaded curtain, Boli and Cristian, Marisol's two little brothers, seemed frightened.

"The police searched?" Marley asked as she entered the kitchen. "That's good."

Mrs. Poveda, who was as petite as her daughter, drew up in surprise.

"The harder they look, the clearer it will be that Marisol was a victim in this crime," Marley insisted. "They'll know what we know: that she is not a thief."

Short too but thick and muscular, with skin as red as it was brown, Mr. Poveda listened as his wife translated. When she was finished, he bowed his head as if to hide a tear, but then he looked at his wife and spoke in Spanish.

Marisol translated. "'By then, my daughter will be sent to prison and our family's reputation will be destroyed.'"

Marley held up the envelope Ben Rosenberg had given her.

"Let's watch this," she said. "I'll bet we'll be able to see something that will help the police understand what really happened."

Marisol stood as her parents talked in rapid-fire Spanish.

Though she understood maybe every third word, Marley felt she got the drift of what the Povedas were saying:

The New York City police are *not* going to listen to a fourteen-year-old girl who thinks she is a detective.

"We'll see," Marley said confidently. "Right is right, after all. In any language."

Mr. and Mrs. Poveda looked at each other with surprise. Marisol managed a small, sorrowful smile.

The apartment's living room had been converted to a bedroom/rehearsal space for Marisol. Her violin was on the bed—Marley assumed the police had examined it—and her beloved cell phone, a gift from her parents, was in its charger. As Marisol quickly tidied her room, Marley slipped the DVD into the player. Mr. Poveda leaned against the door frame, the red and orange beads draping along the back of his steel-blue work shirt.

Mrs. Poveda shooed away the boys as she sat on the bed.

"Let's see if we can find the part with Marisol first," Marley said.

According to the player, the DVD was five hours long. Though she jumped ahead, it still took Marley almost five minutes to find the right part of the security video.

As Mr. and Mrs. Poveda stared at the small screen, Marisol seemed to shuffle in place on the orange throw rug.

"Okay . . . ," Marley said.

Sitting cross-legged, her back against the bed, she narrated the action as she had in her own kitchen, and didn't have to do much to prove her first point: When Marisol appeared on the screen, Mr. and Mrs. Poveda exchanged a curious glance that seemed to say *that* girl wasn't their daughter, but a blank-faced robot that looked and dressed like her.

"Okay, so that's not the Marisol we know," Marley said, tapping the pause button on the remote. Turning to her friend, she added, "Now pick up your violin."

Marisol eased her palm under the instrument's lacquered back before slipping her left hand under its neck. Teddy was right: Marisol cradled the violin as if it were a baby.

"Can you carry it out into the corridor?"

To Marley's surprise, Marisol tucked the violin under her arm. But she saw she had nestled its back gently against her ribs, far from her belt, her hand cupped around its waist.

Looking at Mrs. Poveda and her husband, she said, "Now watch."

The DVD resumed, and a moment later, Marisol's mother said, "It's not the same. No, she's very rough to it."

She repeated her words to her husband in Spanish.

Mr. Poveda drew his daughter near.

"But now," Marley said, "we have to find out what really happened."

And for the next two hours, Marley and Marisol watched a very dull movie: one with lots of characters who milled about and studied a violin, or walked by as if it wasn't there.

Mrs. Poveda fed them *patacones,* the Ecuadorian version of fried plantains. Boli and Cristian went off to bed. Mr. Poveda turned on the Spanish-language broadcast of the Mets game on the kitchen radio, but his endless pacing suggested he was too worried to listen.

"You know, Marley," Marisol whispered. "I think I would remember if I ever had such a special instrument in my hands."

"That's gives me an idea," Marley replied. "Instead of us both watching this, why don't you find out what you can about the violin. Check Juilliard's website, and the *Times'.* They probably have a bunch of stories about it."

As Marisol sat at her PC, copying-and-pasting information into a Word document, Marley studied black-and-white TV. By now, she was fighting boredom and speeding up things with the fast-forward button.

"You'd think one of us would recognize somebody walking through Juilliard," she said, stifling a yawn as she stretched across Marisol's bed. "I'll bet we've seen three hundred people—Wait!"

"What?" Marisol jumped from her chair.

Shifting her thumb on the remote, Marley stopped the action and quickly hit the reverse button. Then she hit stop again.

And there, staring at the $500,000 violin, was, of all people, their algebra teacher, Mr. Noonan.

"I can't believe this," Marisol said.

Now she and Marley were standing side by side in front of the TV monitor.

They let the security video play at normal speed.

Mr. Noonan stared at the violin for nearly five minutes.

He made notes on index cards.

He took out a small digital camera and snapped photos.

He nodded politely at the security personnel.

"Mr. Noonan," Marisol uttered.

"Boring Mr. Noonan," Marley said, shaking her head in wonder.

"You don't think . . . ?"

"I *won't* think," she said. "Not before I talk to someone I know can help us."

chapter 4

When Marley left the Povedas' apartment, she found Teddy leaning against a parking meter outside the redbrick building. Coincidentally, he was reading his algebra textbook, fending off the night's darkness to study by using the glow from the bay window of a pizza parlor. The scent of tart tomato sauce drifted over the avenue.

"How long?—"

Teddy stepped away from the meter. "The dishes are done," he replied as he hitched up his sagging jeans. "How's Marisol?"

"Upset," Marley replied. "But I think now she believes there's a chance we can—"

"Keep her from going to prison?"

"—help clear her name." If there was a police officer watching the Povedas' building, Marley couldn't see him.

They started south, passing crowded outdoor cafés. Diners' conversation and laughter filled the surprisingly cool September air.

"Where are we going?" Teddy had to trot to keep up with Marley's rapid pace.

"Antonio's," she replied.

"You think Miss Otto is there?"

Marley's dreadlocks jiggled as she walked. "If she's not at the restaurant, her father will call her for us."

"I guess. . . ."

In the distance were the lights of Lincoln Center.

They continued in silence and, after going a half-mile or so, arrived at a quiet stretch of the avenue where the shops and boutiques had already closed. Soon, the bustle was well behind them.

As they crossed 81st Street, they approached the long, narrow park behind the American Museum of Natural History. Big leafy trees seemed to quiver in the streetlamps' violet light.

With its menacing towers and turrets, and all the peculiar angles caused by different sorts of buildings being thrown together over the years, the museum complex could seem eerie during the day. At night, it was even scarier, as if the ghosts of its stuffed animals were prowling and slinking around its empty corridors, ready to burst into the street.

At least it seemed that way to Teddy, who refused to glance into the shadows.

Clutching his textbook, he scurried to catch up to Marley, his old Adidas high-tops scraping on cobblestone. Wait, he wanted to shout, the Otto family's restaurant wasn't going anywhere.

Marley turned and held her finger to her lips.

Teddy stopped.

Dark, foreboding music from a violin filled the avenue with sound that seemed to match the threat posed by the scary museum.

Staring toward gray trees, the two friends stood motionless as the music continued, rocketing high as if escaping a monster's grip. Then it swooped down, stopping just short of smashing into the cobblestone.

Then, suddenly, there was silence. A man spun from behind a gnarled tree trunk.

Startled, Teddy bellowed, "Marley!"

The tall, disheveled man marched toward them, holding out his bow as if it were a lance.

The little white envelope Ben Rosenberg had given her fell from Marley's grasp.

"You must pay!" the man shouted. "You listen, you must pay!"

It was Tabakovic, the violinist who they'd seen a few weeks ago on Fifth Avenue outside the Met.

"Run, Marley!" Teddy screamed.

Tabakovic arched his back, shook his head furiously, and roared like an angry bear.

Teddy grabbed Marley's hand. "Let's go!"

"Wait," Marley insisted, yanking her friend back. She groped the cobblestones to retrieve the fallen envelope that held the DVD of the security tape.

Then she dashed off with Teddy, even as Tabakovic continued to howl for payment.

When they'd run about fifty feet up the block, Marley released Teddy's hand.

Turning, she shouted, "Hey Tabakovic! Is that a new violin?"

Gasping, Teddy warned, "Marley . . ."

She barked, "Maybe you don't need your old one anymore."

But now, Tabakovic had stopped growling. He dropped his arms to his sides, his bow and instrument hanging low.

Then, as he began to walk back to his dark perch, he raised his hands again and began to play a tender melody, one that seemed to speak of a deep, lasting sadness.

Listening, Marley and Teddy watched until Tabakovic, and the anguished music, disappeared.

Catching their breath, Marley and Teddy continued south until, once again, they reached the crowded restaurants and cafés on another well-lit strip of Columbus Avenue.

~

The problem for the Kingston Cowboys was they had no place to practice.

Well, as they'd soon find out, that was *one* of their problems.

They'd be too loud to practice at anyone's apartment, and Marley knew her dad liked to work in the evenings after Skeets went to sleep. They couldn't ask their teachers at Beacon or Collegiate if they could use an empty classroom after hours. Half of the band didn't attend whichever school they'd choose. And anyway no one would let kids rattle around the buildings at night, lugging in musical instruments and equipment.

With thousands and thousands of professional musicians living in its five boroughs, New York City was filled with rehearsal halls, but they were expensive. Believe it or not, some bands actually practiced in those mini-storage places where people cram in all the things they can't fit in their apartments, like luggage and old sofas and crummy paintings and footlockers tied with old leather belts. Teddy said he'd heard a senior at Collegiate had rented one down on Spring Street where his band kept their equipment, including the drum kit and amplifiers. They'd squeeze in, turn on the electricity and start rehearsing, though they could hardly move and their heads almost banged the ceiling.

They could chip in their allowance money, Teddy suggested, but Wendell thought he had a better, less costly idea. He proposed it the next afternoon as they sat in a booth at their coffee shop on Broadway.

"There's room in my uncle's basement," he said. "It's where I store my drums."

"Your uncle who was the carnival barker?" Marisol asked.

"That was his grandfather," Teddy said. He turned to Wendell. "Your uncle used to work security at the Lincoln Center jazz hall, right?"

Teddy and Marisol were drinking iced coffee, so Wendell did

too. Marley always ordered the *avgolemono* soup, which was sort of like the Greek version of egg-drop soup. The little bit of lemon in the broth made it incredibly delicious.

"He must've heard some cool music," Marley said.

The Collegiate boys wore jackets, shirts with collars and neck-ties. Marley noticed that whenever she addressed Wendell, who was always so well groomed, he clutched the length of his tie, tugging and squeezing it nervously.

"He's a doorman," he said, "and there's this storage shed . . ."

"What's the address?" Marley asked, taking a sip of the hot soup. No matter that it was ninety degrees outside. This soup was fantastic!

Stroking his tie, Wendell answered her question.

"I know that one," Marley said. "That's a great old place."

West End Avenue was filled with magnificent limestone and terra-cotta apartment buildings, some of which seemed like monuments in the midday sun. Tall and broad, they had aw-nings and fancy ornamentation and gold revolving doors and uniformed doormen who knew everybody who lived inside. The doormen kept things moving and did all sorts of chores, from accepting packages to holding babies while new moms strug-gled with strollers, and helping the handymen as emergency plumbers and carpenters. All that in addition to providing secu-rity by watching over the lobby.

Wendell said, "I'll ask my uncle if we can meet there."

"Well," Marley said, "that ought to get us started."

"It's sort of under the elevator, though . . . ," he added as his cheeks began to turn red again. "And in the winter, there's the furnace."

"No, it's good," Marley said.

Wendell seemed relieved. The move across the river to New York City ripped him from his old friends—which is what his mother and uncle had wanted—and made him more insecure than simply being a gangly teenager ever did.

"When do we start?" Marisol asked.

The answer? Eight days later, on a Friday right after the first week of school ended.

Wendell set up his congas and high-hat cymbal inside the cramped shed, which was bloated with cartons of all different shapes and sizes, and a few rolled-up rugs. Seated just outside the tight space, Marley fed her guitar through a small amplifier, one about the same size Teddy was using for his electric bass. To start, they turned it way down low.

Marisol also stood outside the shed. They weren't sure if the first-floor tenants would be able to hear them, but they figured if Marisol's sweet violin reached upstairs, maybe they wouldn't complain.

Marisol was the only Kingston Cowboy who could really play her instrument.

"Teddy . . . ," Marley chuckled.

The electric bass seemed to cover Teddy's entire chest and stomach, blocking the view of his old Boston Bruins hockey jersey. He could hardly get his arms in place or his plump fingers around the bass's long, long neck.

"I've been practicing," he replied.

Me too, Marley thought. *Maybe if I live to be a hundred, I might know what I'm doing.*

"Want to try something?" Wendell asked. He was deep in the shed, surrounded by crates on the old wooden shelves. A bare lightbulb hung over his head.

"Like what?" Marley asked.

Perplexed, they looked at each other.

Then they started to laugh.

"Is there any song we all know how to play?" Marisol asked. As she spoke, she continued to practice scales, her tiny fingers gliding effortlessly along the violin's neck and strings.

Wendell spoke up. "Well, reggae has its roots in American pop, and American pop has a lot of country music in it. We should be able to find something."

Marley was impressed.

Wendell began playing a simple reggae beat, tapping the side of the conga on the first and third beats, and the drum skin and high-hat on the two and four. He used his fingertips, keeping the rhythmic sound soft.

Teddy stared at his fingers as they waited above the bass's thick strings. He knew it was his turn to enter.

"Try a single note on the one and three," Wendell suggested.

"The key of G," Marisol added.

Biting his bottom lip, Teddy began.

Now Marley faced a problem. So much reggae music was in minor keys, and most country was in majors. She didn't know whether to play G minor or G major.

She thought, *Well, Bob Marley's "I Shot the Sheriff" is in a minor key. . . .*

She played a chopping minor chord, accenting the second and fourth beats.

Soon, Marisol played a beautiful melody that drifted over the rhythm.

A glance passed among the four friends. They seemed to realize they weren't half-bad, at least for the moment.

"Let's shift to C minor," Marisol said, as she continued to play.

Wendell counted, "Two, three . . ."

Marley and Teddy immediately lost their place and the music stopped.

"That," Marley said, "was not good."

"Sorry . . . ," Teddy added.

They returned to the basement a week later, having spent several meetings at the coffee shop discussing and selecting a single song to learn.

They finally chose Stevie Wonder's "Send One Your Love." After downloading it and sharing the file, they concluded that, though maybe it was a bit too old school, it was clear Wonder wrote a pretty great song. Marisol said his compositions were so well constructed that they could easily be stripped down to a country-reggae style.

She arranged the song and wrote the chords on music-notation paper.

When he took his sheet, covered with musical staves and Marisol's neat printing, Teddy realized he felt like a real musician. It drove him to practice extra hard during the week.

His confidence growing, he invited Bassekou to the rehearsal.

The two Collegiate students made an odd couple as they arrived on West End Avenue to meet the three Kingston Cowboys under the awning of Wendell's uncle's building. Teddy wore a Green Bay Packers jersey with the number 08, baggy red nylon shorts and his floppy old Adidas sneakers, the laces flapping. Bassekou, who towered over his new American friend, was in a perfect navy-blue suit, white shirt and blue silk tie.

"Ready?" Wendell said, as he settled behind his drums.

Marisol reached to her belt to shift her cell phone to vibrate.

In a black short-sleeved top, wrinkled parachute pants, and black flip-flops, Marley strapped on her instrument and plucked at the strings with a plastic pick. Holding back her hair, she looked down at the music sheet she had placed at her feet.

"Let's give it our best," Marisol said with cheer.

Wendell snapped his fingers. "One, two, three . . ."

Seconds later, they stopped.

"Sorry," Teddy said. His confidence fled as soon as Wendell began his countdown, and he made his entrance on a very sour note.

Marley smiled at him. "We'll get it, Ted. Not to worry."

They started the song again, and then stopped.

Bassekou shifted uncomfortably. He was eager to learn all he could about Western music and Teddy's enthusiasm had him expecting a level of excellence.

"That's on me," Marley said. The opening chord—a Gbmaj7—was a difficult one for a beginner guitarist.

After the fifth false start, Marisol suggested she play the song through with Wendell tapping out a reggae rhythm.

In her talented hands, the music was lovely, like a beautiful butterfly fluttering around the dank basement.

Marley told her so. Teddy did too.

Smiling, Bassekou said, "Marisol, that was so very sweet. You have a gift. . . ."

He stopped when he realized the Kingston Cowboys were looking past him. When he turned, he saw a man in a burgundy suit jacket with gold braiding, a white shirt and a gray clip-on tie. The man's gray slacks had a black stripe down the side. He carried a burgundy hat with a black plastic visor, and Bassekou saw that the hat had the apartment building's address printed in gold on its front.

He also saw that the thin, pale man seemed to be glaring at Marley, Teddy and Marisol.

"Wendell," the man said. He crooked his finger angrily.

Wendell hurried around the drums, a worried expression on his face.

Marley and Teddy exchanged a quick glance. They both noticed how Wendell's uncle looked at them. It was as if they didn't meet his approval.

Wendell returned three minutes later. Sheepishly, he said, staring at the concrete floor, "We have to go."

"Wendell . . . ?" Marisol said gently. She had cradled her violin under her arm.

"I'm sorry," he replied, refusing to meet her eyes. "But we have to go."

Marley and Teddy headed for their instruments' cases.

"Have we offended your uncle?" Bassekou asked.

Wendell didn't reply. He went inside the shed and began to put away his cymbal and drum.

chapter 5

"Marley Z!" Antonio Otto said with a beaming smile.

Everyone in the narrow restaurant turned to see the commotion.

Miss Otto's father cupped Marley's cheeks, a gesture that instantly swept aside thoughts of the annoying Tabakovic jumping out of the Natural History bushes at her moments earlier.

"How are you? *Molto felice*, I hope."

Mr. Otto seemed to do everything at the restaurant: greet his customers, bring them to one of his eight tables, deliver fresh bread and herb olive oil, take their orders, and then cook and serve all the food. As if to symbolize his many roles, Mr. Otto wore a chef's top—with his name Antonio in script on the breast—and flawless suit pants and shiny Italian loafers that were suitable for the owner of a popular and successful business.

To enter, Teddy sidestepped through the crowd waiting to be seated.

"Ah. Mr. Teddy."

Mr. Otto made a theatrical wave of his hand and bowed at the waist.

The air in Antonio's was scented with a trace of fresh-cooked seafood. On the blackboard near the open kitchen was tonight's menu featuring *Risotto ai Frutti di Mare*—Seafood Risotto. Teddy thought of Mr. Otto's tender clams, shrimp and squid nestled amid buttery rice. He almost groaned with pleasure.

If Marley's father could cook like Mr. Otto . . .

"Is your daughter here, Mr. Otto?" Marley said.

"Vivi?" he replied.

Marley knew he only had one daughter. "Yes."

She didn't mind being part of Mr. Otto's show. Though people in the neighborhood knew him as a tough business-man, to Marley he was always gentle and kind. The bright-eyed man with olive skin and gray razor-cut hair once said her smile made him smile.

"In the office," he said. "You go. Teddy, you too."

He patted Teddy on the head.

Teddy gritted his teeth. He hated to be patted on the head.

At least this time Mr. Otto hadn't scrunched his chubby cheeks.

———

What?" Miss Otto said.

"Do you think Mr. Noonan would steal a violin?" Marley repeated.

Miss Otto spun the swivel chair to face her. An old-style calculator with a hand crank sat on her father's desk in the crowded office and storage space. A new MacBook was next to the creaky machine.

"Absolutely not," she replied. "What are you saying, Marley?"

"How can you be so sure?"

Miss Otto paused.

Teddy, who stood by the door, watched as her expression turned from anger to curiosity.

"Marley," she said pensively, "you've learned something. . . ."

Marley handed her the DVD. "Watch the third hour," she said. "You can start at three-twenty or so."

"Mr. Noonan is on it?" Miss Otto asked. She slipped the white envelope into her book bag at the side of the desk.

Yes, Marley thought as she nodded. *Boring old Mr. Noonan.*

"I shouldn't be surprised," Miss Otto said. "Ira Noonan collects violins. American violins."

"Mr. Noonan?"

Marley couldn't imagine him doing anything but pacing slowly in front of the green board, moan-droning on and on about variables and equations, chalk dust on his jacket and slacks.

"The violin that was stolen was made in America, wasn't it?" Miss Otto asked.

"The Habishaw. Yes, in Massachusetts," Marley said. "In 1873."

Miss Otto smiled at the flash of certainty her father so admired in young Marley Zimmerman.

"You still don't believe Marisol took it, do you?" Miss Otto asked.

"I know she *took* it," Marley replied. "But something—or someone—made her."

Teddy listened as Marley explained what she'd seen on the security video.

When she was finished, she said, "Can you ask Mr. Noonan if he can help us?"

"Marley, tomorrow you can—"

"Can you call him now?"

"Now? I suppose. . . ."

"I'll meet him early," she said.

Miss Otto reached for the old black phone on the desk.

"Thank you," Marley said.

As she waited for Mr. Noonan to answer, Miss Otto asked, "How's Collegiate, Teddy?"

"Good," Teddy nodded. "Fine."

"I'm glad," she smiled. "But we're sorry you're not with us."

Beacon was one of the best public high schools in the city, if not the whole country. But a private school like Collegiate meant something to Teddy's parents. Founded in 1628, it not only offered a great education. To Mr. and Mrs. So, it seemed to symbolize America and its brightest hopes and values.

Miss Otto turned. "Ira?" she said into the black handset. "This is Vivianna Otto. I'm sorry to bother you at home, but I

have a request"—she looked at Marley—"and it seems urgent."
Marley rocked on her heels and smiled.

*T*he following morning, Marley leafed through the *New York Times* as she waited for Mr. Noonan on Amsterdam Avenue across from the back of Damrosch Park. Still no mention of the theft of the Habishaw violin, and nothing more about the tiny fire that had disrupted Juilliard. The news on WNYC, the public radio station her father loved, hadn't talked about the Habishaw either, nor did she find anything about it on the Web, except for something in a gossipy blog written by a classical music fan on the Upper West Side. The blogger speculated that the Habishaw was in storage until the Lincoln Center experts assessed the smoke damage.

Maybe the police didn't want to say anything about their search for the missing violin. Marley remembered how Sgt. Sampson pushed Marisol to reveal where she had taken it. Finding that violin was his priority, and the pressure of publicity might force whoever had it to do something desperate. That might explain the silence.

Mr. Noonan came through the park, the morning sun over his shoulder, walking no faster than he did at the front of his classroom. Marley was surprised to see him smiling.

"Shall we?" he said as he drew next to her. His green corduroy jacket was wrinkled, and the plaid tie against his yellow shirt was way off center.

Marley tucked the newspaper under her arm and, hoisting the handle of the rolling luggage she used for a book bag, followed Mr. Noonan west on 61st Street.

He led her up the steps and to the school library.

As Marley nestled in a seat, her back to the tall stacks of books, Mr. Noonan reached into his leather satchel and pulled out a Polaroid photo.

"That's it. The Habishaw violin," he said, as he sat across from her. "The woodworking is thoroughly characteristic of the Boston School. See the purfling and the flame? The tapering of the tailpiece . . . ? Also, that's not the original Habishaw chin rest, which was replaced in the 1920s."

Marley mentioned that display case was different from the one she'd seen in the security video.

"I took that photo at the Fiske Museum in California. At Claremont College," he said. "Do you know it? What a wonderful museum. An amazing collection of rare instruments, surely one of the most impressive in the United States."

Marley looked at her teacher. She couldn't believe it: He glowed with excitement and enthusiasm.

"As for American instruments, they have a John Sellers piano made in the late Eighteenth Century; a Boston Musical Instrument Manufactory from . . . ah . . . 1871, I think it is; a David Hall circular cornet; a saxello, a Conn-O-Sax . . ."

He paused.

"But you were asking about stringed instruments."

In fact, Marley hadn't asked a question. "Someone stole the Habishaw violin," she said.

"Yes, our Marisol," Mr. Noonan replied. "Or so I'm told."

"But she was someone's agent," she said, holding up her hand. "An unwitting agent. I'm sure of it!"

Marley sat back. She wore an old navy-blue service station uniform top with a flying red horse insignia. Her father found it at an antique-clothes shop in Pittsburgh. It was way too big, but it was also too great just to hang in the closet.

"'Unwitting.' Meaning 'involuntary' or 'unsuspecting,'" Mr. Noonan said thoughtfully.

"I know," Marley said. "My father uses that expression all the time in the Time Traveler. She was an unwitting agent."

"Marisol Poveda doesn't strike me as a thief," Mr. Noonan mused. "But I've been fooled before. . . ."

"You're not being fooled this time," Marley insisted. "Somebody made her do it."

Mr. Noonan edged forward in his seat. "A threat?"

Marley said no. "She didn't seem nervous or anything. She wasn't looking over her shoulder."

They sat in silence for a moment, as if they were trying to think of how Marisol could have been tricked into stealing a valuable instrument.

"At any rate," Mr. Noonan said, tapping his finger on the Polaroid. "The Habishaw, or the 'bloodstained violin' as it's known, must be returned."

And so," Marley said over her steamy bowl of lemony Greek soup, "Mr. Noonan confirmed what we learned online. The bloodstained violin was built by Nehemiah Habishaw, who was born in Poland, but he came to America when he was a kid."

Teddy and Wendell listened attentively, water tears sliding along their tall glasses of iced coffee.

Marisol's seat in the booth was empty, just as her desk had been at Beacon.

"He was associated with what they called the Boston School of violin makers," she continued, hand resting on her spoon. "Lots of great violins were made in America—in New York, Chicago, Philadelphia. The people who made them were tremendous craftsmen. You see all sorts of detail in the woodwork. Really beautiful."

She took a sip of the hot soup.

"What makes the Habishaw so valuable is . . . Well, there are a few things. One is it's the only one he made that's left. Nobody used to pay too much attention to American-made violins, so I guess people didn't really take care of them, or collect them. Or they played them until they wore out. Almost every household in America used to have a violin."

"Did people think the European ones were better?" Teddy asked.

Marley nodded. "The ones made by Stradivari or Guarneri. They studied under Amati, who started in, like, 1650. There are a few made by Stradivari still around," she continued. "From 1664 or so. But, yeah, only one Habishaw."

"The other reasons . . . ?" Teddy asked.

"The bloodstain," she replied.

"Real blood?" asked Wendell.

"No, no," Marley said. "But there's a red blemish in the maple under one of the F-holes that sort of looks like a blood drop. It's kind of hard to see at first, but it's there: a red blood drop."

"In the wood, not the varnish?" Teddy asked.

"Right in the wood," Marley nodded. "But the most important thing about the Habishaw is the way it sounds. Apparently, it's, like, so beautiful. Mr. Noonan said it sounded like the voice of a special angel who descends from heaven only when someone plays it. Something about the wood or the way it was cared for and repaired or how it aged. It had some sort of blessed life."

Teddy frowned. "So someone who loves the sound of a violin and loves to play—"

"Mr. Noonan said there's no way a violinist worthy of the Habishaw took it. The kind of people who could play it well enough to create that beautiful sound don't go around stealing instruments."

Not quite convinced, Teddy said, "All right . . ."

"A better way to think of it is to imagine that five hundred thousand dollars was sitting under that display case," Marley said.

"So the thief needs to find someone who'll buy it for a lot of money," Teddy said. "Maybe not the full five hundred thousand, but a *lot*."

"Bang," Marley replied, pointing at him with her spoon.

"So it's a collector who would buy stolen goods," Wendell said. He dropped another cube of brown sugar into his drink. He didn't exactly enjoy iced coffee unless it was super sweet.

"I'd bet that's who the police are looking for," Teddy added. "They're probably following Marisol and her mother and father. . . ."

In her mind, Marley finished Teddy's comment: to see if the Povedas would take the Habishaw out of hiding and turn it over to a crooked dealer or collector.

Calling on her cell, Marley spoke to Marisol four times today, promising to e-mail her the homework assignments and drop off her books, if necessary. But, mostly, she called to be a friend: Sgt. Sampson interviewed Marisol again, this time with her parents and their attorney at the 20th Precinct. It was awful, Marisol reported the first time Marley called. Humiliating. Terrifying.

"But the person I need to find isn't just a crooked dealer or collector who would accept a stolen violin," Marley said to Teddy and Wendell. "The police are on to that, I'm sure. I need to find the person who could get Marisol to be his agent. His unwitting agent."

"Is there a collector who could do that?" Wendell asked.

"A facilitator," Teddy proposed. "A go-between."

"Maybe," Marley said. "I need to talk to someone who knows all kinds of collectors and dealers."

They sat in silence as Marley finished her soup.

As always, when Teddy reached the bottom of his glass, his straw made a ghastly slurping sound and, as always, he laughed like a happy child.

"Hey, Marley," Wendell ventured. "Your Mr. Noonan was pretty helpful, wasn't he?"

She nodded. "I'm kind of sorry I told you guys he was so

boring," she replied. "Turns out there's more to him than I recognized."

"Well, that happens," he replied agreeably.

Teddy said, "Sometimes there's less than you recognize too."

"With people, you never know," Marley said.

~

As he waited patiently in the Monday morning shadows on the corner of 84th and Columbus, Teddy's thoughts were still troubled by the abrupt end to band practice on Friday.

For the moment, though, his mind wandered. Leaving his luggage book bag in the shade, his Collegiate jacket hanging on its handle, he took a few steps into the sun and, arching his back, looked straight up past the building's tarred cornice to study the sky. It'll be a hot day, he told himself; hot and sticky. The kind that's superfantastic in August when you can hang out with your friends in Riverside Park, coconutty lotion on your nose and cheeks, the breeze wafting off the Hudson. Or jumping in the pool at the Chelsea Rec Center. Teddy knew he sort of slapped at the water, laughing as he tried to keep up with Marley, chlorine turning his eyes pink. As for Marisol, she said she learned to swim in the Pacific Ocean. She zipped through the turquoise water like a dolphin. . . .

Lost in blissful memories not yet a month old, Teddy, at least for a moment, forgot his concerns and why he was waiting on the busy avenue when he should be on his way to school. Then he saw his friend.

"Wendell!" he shouted.

Wearing his new blue backpack, lunch sack in hand, Wendell Justice walked along the sunny west side of the avenue. His jacket was neat, his shirt pressed, his tie tight to the collar.

He looked up, saw Teddy, but then kept going.

Between them, taxis zoomed by as if they were in a NASCAR race.

Teddy waited for the traffic light to change—from "Hand to Man," as Marley would've said. Then, his book bag bouncing and bumping behind him, Teddy jogged across the soon-to-be soupy asphalt.

"Wendell," he said as he lugged his bag over the curb, "what's going on?"

"Hi, Teddy," he replied dourly, his cheeks turning red.

"We didn't see you this weekend."

Wendell hadn't stopped moving. He seemed in a rush to get to Collegiate, which was a few blocks away on 78th Street, not too far from the Natural History Museum.

"Yeah . . . I got caught up in a few things," replied Wendell, as he looked into the distance.

"I called, I texted . . ."

"I know."

The rushing crowd around them headed toward the office towers up ahead at Columbus Circle and beyond.

Teddy decided to be bold. Looking up at Wendell, he said, "Nobody minds. It was nice of you to try to get us a place to rehearse. If your uncle—"

"Listen, Ted," Wendell said abruptly. "I've got to—I've got to go."

With that, he started to rush as fast as he could, moving quickly away from Teddy.

Flabbergasted, Teddy wanted to shout to his friend. Instead, he just stood there, fists on his hips, people charging by, cars and delivery vans too.

Teddy looked terribly confused.

chapter 6

Dad, I'm going to the Met to see a curator!" Marley shouted, her words smooshing together as she hurried for the vestibule, baby sister jiggling on her hip. "I've got Skeeter and we'll be home for dinner. Bye."

Marley was already over on Central Park West, hand in the air to flag a taxicab when her father, struggling over the latest Time Traveler adventure, said, "Bye." He glanced at his cell phone. Most days, it was his link to his family, except Skeeter who was too young for a real cell phone, but had a little pink plastic one she loved to chew.

Taking 86th Street across Central Park, the yellow cab rode under green-black leaves, passing chestnut and red horses on the bridle path, and dropped the Zimmerman girls on 84th Street, just a short walk from the Met.

"Up, Skeets," Marley said, as she put the change in her jeans pocket.

Diaper showing beneath her lavender shorts, Skeeter struggled into the portable stroller, which was about the size of an umbrella before it was opened. As she sat, she adjusted her blue Time Traveler bucket hat, the Trylon and Persiphere from the 1939 New York World's Fair on the front.

Marley dumped her notebook in the stroller's little basket.

"The appointment's for three o'clock," she said, as she buckled her sister in tight. "We've got to move."

She silently thanked Mr. Noonan, who called the museum to set up the meeting, and Miss Otto, who arranged for her to skip her last class.

Up ahead, the museum's long, white steps weren't at all crowded: Most New Yorkers were at work or college or finishing up school for the day or were occupied with one project or another, probably two or three, knowing New Yorkers. The tourists coming down toward Fifth Avenue, guidebooks in their hands, seemed totally contented. With only hundreds of people inside the Met, instead of thousands, they'd had an excellent view of the museum's vast collection.

Skeeter cooed happily and continued to chomp on her bare foot.

———

Bebe Douglass, who had the very cool title of Director of Chordophones, was, like, twenty-five years old and cheery, and probably knew everything about stringed instruments, including the name of the caveman who put together the first one. She made it clear she knew no legitimate collector who would be willing to buy the stolen Habishaw violin, or a reputable dealer who would be willing to sell it. The NYPD, she said, had a long list of corrupt collectors and dealers, and she was certain they'd already been questioned.

As Skeeter sat on the floor in her tiny office behind the Musical Instruments gallery, Ms. Douglass said, "As I told Sgt. Sampson, it breaks my heart to think we may never see the Habishaw again."

"Really?" Marley said. "*Never* again?"

"Whoever stole this violin can't display it, can he?"

"I guess not . . . ," she replied, as she kept her eye on Skeeter, who happily explored the packets of dried soup mix the curator had given her to play with.

"Even if it ends up on display in a private home, Juilliard would find out, the Fiske would too. We certainly would know," Ms. Douglass said. "The world is small, and the world of rare stringed instruments is even smaller."

"And there's only one bloodstained violin," Marley said. "So you think it will just end up in somebody's home?"

"If we're lucky. . . ."

"Lucky?"

"What if someone stole it so they could destroy it?"

Marley hadn't thought of that. "Why?"

Ms. Douglass put her arms on her desk. "Why would they destroy it? Or why would they steal it?"

Marley thought for a moment and then a moment more as she lifted Skeeter on to her lap.

"No, it's too valuable to destroy," she said finally and with plenty of conviction.

Ms. Douglass nodded. Ira Noonan had told her that Marley's friend had been accused of the crime—had, in fact, been video-taped removing the instrument from its display case at Juilliard. But, Mr. Noonon had said, Marley believed Marisol was only a pawn being played by the real thief, and he thought so, too.

The curator could feel the power of Marley's conviction, even as she held a giggling baby on her lap.

"Would someone steal it so they could play it?" Marley asked.

She hesitated. "It would take someone with a troubled mind to steal it just to play it, I'm afraid."

The expression "a troubled mind" sparked a thought.

Marley said, "You have a Stradivarius here from—"

"The year 1693," Ms. Douglass replied.

"Do you let people play it?"

Ms. Douglass was surprised by the question. "Very few. By special appointment only."

"Would you let Tabakovic?" Marley asked.

"That angry man who plays on the street? No. Itzhak Perlman, for sure. Nadia Salerno-Sonnenberg, yes."

Marley understood. Whether Tabakovic was dangerous, as Teddy claimed, or just eccentric, the Met couldn't trust a rare Stradivarius to him. Nor would Juilliard allow him to play the Habishaw, even if he'd been a student there once.

Marley shuddered at a vivid impression that crossed her mind: She imagined Tabakovic was playing the Habishaw violin in the park behind the Natural History Museum; suddenly, he raises it and smashes it against a bench or a water fountain, a million shards of beautiful old wood flying everywhere, splinters bouncing onto Columbus Avenue.

If someone like Tabakovic really, really wanted to play a really, really rare violin, he'd have to steal it.

After thanking Ms. Douglass, Marley plopped Skeeter in her stroller and decided to put in a few minutes exploring the gallery. But not too many: She knew she had to make up her last class, do her homework and spend some time with Marisol, if not in person, then online.

But there were 5,000 pieces in the Met's collection of musical instruments from 300 B.C. to today. Five thousand! According to her research, they included a guitar from about 1640 that came from Italy. Marley wanted to see a guitar that was more than 365 years old. She wondered when her electric guitar was made.

The Zimmerman girls proceeded through the gallery, the stroller swerving to avoid ankles. A typical New Yorker, Marley went too fast, storming along when it probably would've been more enjoyable just to stop and study what's on display. But there was so much to see, probably too much, and not just stringed instruments, but crystal flutes and ivory recorders, conch shells and bells, and ancient pianos and harpsichords—sometimes with paintings of the people who owned them on the wall behind them. Everything was presented so beautifully.

Marley and Skeeter headed toward the part of the gallery that held instruments from Africa—an ennanga from Uganda, a kind of xylophone from Mozamb—

Marley stopped.

Across the quiet room, standing next to a display case was Mahjoob, the man of "mystical powers" who usually sat behind a card table outside the Met in a robe and glittery turban. Today, as she moved quietly to hide behind a wall outside the room, Marley saw he wore a regular old pale-green polo shirt, brown slacks and brown leather sandals over bare feet.

Skeeter let out a happy squeal and, for no reason, started to clap her little hands.

"*Shhh,*" Marley said gently. "Skeets . . ."

Mahjoob was taking instructions from a guy in a black suit, and even from a distance Marley could tell he was listening carefully. They were the only two people in the room.

The guy reached into his pocket.

With hopeful eyes, Mahjoob watched as he withdrew a plump, letter-sized envelope from the inside of his jacket.

Bowing his head in gratitude, Mahjoob accepted the packet.

Without another word, the guy said good-bye and moved toward the exit at the opposite side of the gallery.

When he reached the opening, he turned to address Mahjoob.

Marley saw that the guy in the black suit wasn't a grown adult. He was Bassekou Sissoko, the ambassador's son from Mali who was Teddy's and Wendell's classmate at Collegiate.

He said, "American instruments, Mahjoob. Remember, only American instruments."

"I understand," Mahjoob replied. "As you wish, my young friend."

Marley spun Skeeter and her stroller.

They hid in the gallery next door, behind lovely Japanese screens, until Bassekou and Mahjoob were long gone.

After taxiing from the Met, Marley re-entered the vestibule of her family's brownstone and draped Skeeter's stroller across the hooks atop an old mirror. Pushing raincoats and slickers aside, Marley studied herself in the glass. *Yep,* she thought as she fluffed her hair, *I look totally confused.*

She caught up to her baby sister in the kitchen. Skeeter giggled happily, nestled in her father's arms.

"Marley," he said as she entered, "you look totally confused."

"I need advice," she said.

"Chop the herbs," he said, gesturing to the counter where his array of potted thyme, basil, oregano and rosemary rested. "We'll talk."

A faded Felix the Cat smiled from the front of his equally

faded, once-black T-shirt, which, like most of Zeke Z's clothes, was way too huge for his skinny frame.

She said, "How about I cook and you chop?"

He looked at his daughter. Something, or maybe someone, had taken the spring from her step. "Absolutely," he said. "Let me wash up Skeets and get her in the playpen. . . ."

A few minutes later, as she pulled an eggplant and some baby bella mushrooms from the refrigerator, and selected dried pasta from the cabinet, Marley told her father what had happened in the Musical Instruments gallery.

On the other side of the counter, Zeke Z listened as he carefully opened tiny red peppers he'd grown in his garden. He'd let Marley use their seeds to add a little heat to tonight's meal.

"I guess you can't tell Teddy because he sees Bassekou every day," he said.

"Right. A false accusation would be horrible."

"For sure," he nodded. He used thin Latex gloves when he worked with his peppers. A burn on his fingertips would make drawing, painting and lettering the Time Traveler panels too painful.

"But he did say 'only American instruments.'"

Zeke Z thought for a moment. "Is Bassekou a thief?"

"I don't know," she said as she put the eggplant on the cutting board.

"Well, we know Mahjoob is," he said.

"What I can't figure out is how Marisol could have become an unwitting agent for Mahjoob and Bassekou," Marley said. "I could just ask her."

"Right. Why not?"

Marley put down the knife next to the eggplant. "I'll see if she's online now," she said excitedly.

"Okay. I'll take over the cooking." He began to ease off his gloves.

"No, no. Never mind," Marley said quickly. "I'll IM her after the sauce gets underway and the water boils."

"All right . . . ," he said, returning to his task.

As she picked up the knife and sliced the eggplant into meaty chunks, she realized she felt better for having spoken to her dad. And she was relieved that they would end the long afternoon sharing a dinner made without hurting his feelings.

DreadZ: WU?

Jipijapa: Not much. U?

DreadZ: RUOK?

Jipijapa: Headache. I'm so worried. . . .

DreadZ: ☹

Jipijapa: Thnx. Hwork?

DreadZ: Mucho. Good diversion. CallUL8R.

Jipijapa: K. News?

DreadZ: Some. FWIW, Noonan is GR8.

Jipijapa: WHA?!?!

DreadZ: lol. Yeah. BTW, you talk 2 Mahjoob?

Jipijapa: ??? 5th Ave Mahjoob? No, never.

DreadZ: K. Mystic Mahjoob. Poo.

Jipijapa: Y?

DreadZ: Scoping. DMAF, make a diary of last week.

Jipijapa: No prob. Did 1 for my Ps. & NYPD.

DreadZ: Ps. They K?

Jipijapa: Worried 2.

DreadZ: Itll be awright soon. Emmis.

Jipijapa: Gracias, amiga.

DreadZ: TTYL.

DreadZ: NOONAN IS GR8!

Jipijapa: LOL! Needed that!

chapter 7

Teddy knew Wendell wasn't going to come to the coffee shop, not after the way his new friend ran away from him this morning and avoided him all day.

"He ignored you?" Marisol asked.

Teddy nodded. "In class, in the halls . . . On Columbus Avenue . . ."

"At lunch?" Marley looked up from blowing on her soup.

"I don't know where he ate," Teddy replied. "He wasn't in the cafeteria." He shrugged. "He doesn't know anybody else, to be honest."

"Bassekou?" Marisol suggested.

"Bassekou goes out to lunch," Teddy said. "His father arranges it or something."

"Bad Monday, Ted," Marley said. "Sorry."

"But I don't even know what's happening." His voice inched higher. "I don't blame Wendell for his uncle putting us out. I mean, we stink and all—not you, Marisol—and he's the doorman in charge. He can do what he wants. It's not Wendell's fault."

Marisol ran her finger along the side of the tall icy glass. "That's not it, Teddy," she said. "He just didn't want us there."

Teddy was persistent. "Why?"

"Ted . . . ," Marley warned. She'd thought a lot about this subject over the weekend.

"I don't think we are the kind of kids he wants his nephew to be with," Marisol said.

"Why?"

She edged forward. "You see how neat he dresses? And remember he told us how his mother moved him from New Jersey so he could go to Collegiate?"

"Right . . . ," Teddy said thoughtfully.

"Didn't he tell you his mother told him he was his family's future?" Marisol said. "How his father and his uncle had to work in the carnival as little boys because the family was so very poor?"

"Yes . . ."

Marley said, "And here we are, all ragtag and a mess and we're hanging out in the basement with the spiders, saggy on a Friday after a week of school, especially when it's been ninety degrees every day. . . ."

"Maybe from the outside," Marisol said, "it doesn't look like we are doing so great."

Teddy said, "Yes. But we are. We're all doing great."

Marley smiled.

"We're excellent students. Very diligent," he continued, "and I think . . . Where are you going?"

Marisol was sliding out of the booth, the back of her legs squeaking on vinyl. "I think I will talk to Wendell's uncle."

"Are you sure?" Teddy asked.

Marisol stood next to Marley and her bowl of lemon egg-drop soup.

"I introduced Wendell to our group," she said, glancing at the clock in her cell phone. "It is my responsibility."

A few minutes passed with Marley and Teddy in silence, save for the clicking of her spoon on the bottom of the bowl.

Teddy wondered if he'd done something wrong. He felt as if he had chased Marisol to her task.

"It's fine, Ted," Marley said, almost reading his mind. "She would've done it anyway. That's Marisol."

Relieved, he decided to change the conversation.

"That cell phone, huh?" he said with a forced chuckle. "She really loves it."

"Her parents gave it to her for her birthday."

"Notice how she's got it programmed to ring something different for each caller?"

Marley nodded.

"Do you know what your song is?" he asked.

"How could I?" she replied. "I mean, I'm not around when I call her."

Teddy paused. "No, I guess not."

He fell back into his thoughts.

Then he said, "Think I should start ironing my hockey jerseys?"

When Marley laughed, Teddy did too.

Marisol arrived on West End Avenue to find Wendell's uncle entertaining two young children who had just jumped to the curb from the back of a shiny black limousine.

The excited kids, who had dropped their colorful school backpacks to the sidewalk, giggled as the doorman seemed to make a coin appear out of thin air. Then he made it vanish again. Seconds later, he found it—in the little girl's ear.

"Give it to me," she said, laughing.

Her brother clapped his hands in delight.

"Do it again!" the little boy demanded.

The limousine driver stood at attention at the side of the car.

A young woman in navy slacks and a sleeveless top was waiting under the awning.

"That's enough, Nicholas," the woman said.

Wendell's uncle turned. "Yes, ma'am," he said, touching the bill of his cap with a long finger. "My apologies, ma'am."

The woman unfolded her arms to shoo her two children inside the building.

"Good-bye, Tommy," the doorman said, retrieving the backpacks. "Good-bye, Wendy."

Moments later, Marisol entered the vast air-conditioned lobby of the beautiful building. She looked around, and saw that halfway to the elevators, several brown-leather sofas faced a huge fireplace that had over it a long, musty painting of an old-time foxhunt.

Mr. Justice was seated on a high swiveling chair at his small, boxy station just off the vestibule. What looked like one of those old-fashioned switchboards was on the wall to his right. A goose-neck lamp shone a bright light on the Arts section of the *New York Times*, which was covered in part by a stack of some kind of memo from management. Marisol imagined he had to give one to each of the tenants, or maybe put one in each mailbox.

"Hello," she said politely.

Mr. Justice nodded tiredly toward a sign-in sheet on the station's ledge."I'm Marisol Poveda," she said. "Wendell's friend." When her name didn't register with the doorman, she added, "I play the violin."

Mr. Justice stood, his eyes widening. "Oh yes," he said. "The violin."

Marley struggled with her homework. She did her essay and completed the geography assignment easily enough. But algebra was a nightmare. Boring Mr. Noonan's boring question: Which four consecutive numbers, when added together, total eighteen?

Easy. Three, four, five and six.

But how to express it in a word problem?

And why?

"Dad!"

"Can't help you, Marley," he shouted. He was giving Skeeter a splashy bath. Soap bubbles floated into the hall.

She speed-dialed Teddy.

"Ha!" he said. "It's so simple. . . ."

Easy for him, she thought, as she hung up the phone. He was good at math, though he wasn't the genius his father demanded.

She tried Wendell via e-mail, really just to see if he'd reply. He didn't.

Finally, Marisol.

"Mr. Justice apologized," she reported, "and he was nice. Very nice."

"Really?" Marley was lying on the bedroom floor, her long legs and bare feet up on the bed. On her desk, her algebra book was propped open against her computer monitor. Scrap paper surrounded her wastebasket.

"He said he would tell Wendell to catch up with Teddy at school," Marisol told her friend. "He didn't know Teddy attended Collegiate too."

Marley smiled as she spun around to sit cross-legged, her back to her floppy, disheveled bed. Now Teddy would be happy again, and shy Wendell would have a friend.

Everybody was happy.

Except her.

That word problem!

Mr. *Noonan*! How could someone so boring be so much trouble!

Marley waited on the top front step a few minutes before midnight. The lights from the window to her father's office shone behind her as he watched her from his perch at his drafting table.

He knew why she was there. "You don't have to explain," he said as he kissed her forehead before she went out. "But don't neglect your sleep."

Marley's father believed every teenager needed ten hours of sleep a night. Said it was a scientific fact. In the Time Traveler, his character Mike Barnett was always drowsing off someplace or another because he didn't get his ten hours a night. No wonder—Mike was sixteen years old and stuck in a time warp between the 1939–40 and 1964–65 New York World's Fairs. He solved crimes in both eras. That was enough to make anybody tired.

And she had to admit that she could use some sleep. Last night's hadn't been very satisfying—she tossed and turned with worry about Marisol—and then she was up early for her meeting with Mr. Noonan. Marley felt that if she stretched out on the brownstone steps, she'd be asleep in seconds, nestled comfortably under the smattering of stars in the night sky.

Instead, she watched as Dr. Gachet wrestled with his French bulldog Claudette, scolding her in their native language. That little cream-colored dog was stubborn, and Marley knew she wouldn't relent until he let her visit Central Park West. A lot of puppies, and big old mutts too, hung around up there on the way to the park.

"Perhaps you would like a dog, Marley?" Dr. Gachet said with a thick French accent. "For you, there is absolutely no charge."

He followed Claudette as she trotted slowly toward the violet streetlights to the east.

Ten minutes later, a black town car pulled in front of the Zimmerman home.

Wrapped in her red hoody, Marley stood to greet it.

ℐs everything all right?" Mrs. Zimmerman asked as she stepped from the backseat.

Marley came down and met her at the curb. She said, "I've got troubles, Mom."

Without a second thought, Althea Fontenot Zimmerman put down her briefcase and took her daughter in her arms.

After the long, satisfying hug ended, Marley said, "Can we use the limo?"

Mrs. Z frowned in curiosity. "I suppose. . . ." She knew her daughter wasn't frivolous. If Marley asked for a limo, Marley needed a limo.

She opened the door and Marley hopped inside, asking the driver to head south along Columbus Avenue toward Lincoln Center.

And then she told her mother about her long, long day. As

she spoke, she used her red sleeve to wipe the lens of her father's mini-binoculars, which had a Time Traveler logo on the focus adjuster.

Mrs. Z recounted, "A meeting with a teacher, a full day of school, a visit to the Met to talk to a curator, seeing your friend Bassekou—"

"I thought he was my friend. *Our* friend."

Mrs. Z dropped her hand on her daughter's thigh. "Let's not be rash, all right?"

Marley turned to look out through the tinted windows. The Juilliard School was on the right, and a handful of people were filtering down the steps of the Walter Reade Theater next door, enriched after seeing a film from Serbia, Namibia, Borneo or some such faraway place. "But Bassekou said 'only American instruments,' Mom."

Mrs. Z had already heard what the boy from Mali said to Mahjoob. Her husband told her when he e-mailed an update.

"So you have several suspects . . . ," she led.

"With that video of Marisol taking the bloodstained violin," Marley replied, "it won't be enough just to say she didn't do it."

Except for a few chatting people who ringed the sprouting fountain, ice-cream cones or coffee cups in hand, the Lincoln Center plaza was empty. The lights behind the arches of the Metropolitan Opera House had already been dimmed to a golden hue.

"Make a right here, please," she said.

"One of your suspects?" Mrs. Z asked, as the car turned.

Stifling a yawn, Marley asked the driver to pull next to Damrosch Park.

A minute or so later, her mother followed her as she headed cautiously along a winding concrete path lined with thick bushes. If they continued to the path's end, they'd wind up at an open space with a band shell used for outdoor concerts.

Trees rich with plump leaves just about blocked out the moon and stars.

"Marley—"

"*Shhh!*" she replied. Whispering, she added, "Those high heels!"

Mrs. Zimmerman wore three-inch heels that perfectly matched her trim dark-brown suit. "Sorry," she said sheepishly.

Even in the dull light of the park, Marley could see her mom was up for the adventure. "Listen," Marley said. "Do you hear it?"

The sound of a gentle Eastern European ballad played on a violin wafted toward them.

"Hunch down," Marley instructed.

The sad, sweet music continued.

"Come on," Marley said.

The two of them proceeded along the shadowy path, their backs like turtle shells as they edged through the darkness, moving closer to the lovely yet melancholy sound.

When they were maybe fifty yards from the band shell, Marley nodded toward a bench. Squirrels scrambled as she and her mom slunk toward it.

They both sat.

"Who is it?" Mrs. Z whispered.

"It's Tabakovic," Marley replied softly. "But the real question is 'What is it?'"

Mrs. Z thought, *There's pain in that music. It sounds like a cry from a broken heart.*

Marley climbed up and stood on the bench, then squatted down. She showed her mother the binoculars.

"Ready?"

Mrs. Z nodded.

Marley raised up quickly, her mother's hand supporting her. She looked through the binoculars.

With her index finger, she focused the lenses.

Tabakovic was standing in front of the band shell. A streetlamp provided a spotlight.

Eyes closed, his body swaying, he continued to play his poignant song.

The binoculars brought Marley so close that she could see the gray stubble on Tabakovic's chin, his frayed shirt collar and the grime under his fingers as they flitted along the violin's narrow neck.

She could also see the instrument's scroll and peg box above that neck. Pale light shone on the violin's soundboard and waist.

"It's not the Habishaw," she said as she stepped down. "No bloodstain."

She handed her mother the binoculars.

As Marley sat, Mrs. Zimmerman stood tall. "That poor man," she moaned as she watched Tabakovic swoon while he played. "That poor, heartsick man."

Marley said, "Let's go, Mom."

They held hands as they left the park.

In her floppy old pajamas, Marley said good night to her parents and retreated to her room. One o'clock was way too late to be up on a school night, but she was satisfied she'd done good work. From Mr. Noonan, she'd learned about rare violins and their history, and Bebe Douglass at the Met confirmed it was unlikely a serious musician had taken it—which, a few hours later, led her to eliminate Tabakovic as a suspect.

Her next step was to find out what Bassekou was up to.

But first, she needed a good night's sleep.

As her head sank in her pillow, Marley stared at the printout of the e-mail attachment Marisol had sent, her diary of the day the Habishaw was stolen.

Marley read it again and again as if there was a secret message hidden in the words.

```
Shower
B'fast
Walk to school on Columbus
Met MZ at school
Classes
Lunch w/ MZ
Classes
Leave for Riverside Dr. for violin lessons
55 w/ Mr. Gabor
```

```
Food shopping
Home at 5:45, as usual—confirmed by my dad
Helped brothers with homework
Cooked dinner
Mom home at 7:15
Dinner
Homework
TV/Online
Bed
```

The note fluttered from Marley's fingers as she nodded off to sleep.

chapter 8

By Tuesday afternoon, all was forgiven.

Everybody agreed Marisol's decision to visit Mr. Justice turned out to be a good idea.

Wendell was no longer snubbing Teddy, as he had yesterday. Teddy's feelings were restored—how much better the world was when he was happy and carefree!

"Wendell was waiting for me this morning on 84th and Columbus," Teddy explained, when he called Marley at lunchtime. "He apologized and said his uncle had a much better appreciation of us. Oh, Marley, his cheeks were all red. . . ."

"Ted . . ."

"Perhaps we shouldn't say anything to him when we meet later."

"Ted . . ."

"Not even about whether we're going to continue to be Kingston Cowboys."

"Ted . . ."

"I'm pretty sure he doesn't know Marisol went to see his uncle—"

"Ted!"

Teddy, who had wandered over to the west side of Broadway to make his call, yanked the phone away from his ear. "What?" he complained.

"I've got algebra in five minutes," she explained. "Look at what I texted you. Please."

He studied his phone's screen. It read $X + (X+1) + (X+2) + (X+3) = 18$.

With stubby thumbs, he typed, "U got it!"

When he put the phone back to his ear, he heard Marley say, "Good news about Wendell, Teddy. See you at the coffee shop."

After signing off, Teddy waited for a Zabar's van to pass, then started back toward Collegiate.

Three hours later, he was waiting with Wendell in their booth when Marley arrived.

"Where's Marisol?" Wendell asked.

Marley noticed he'd loosened his tie and unbuttoned his top collar.

"She has a violin lesson," she replied as she slid in, her denim shorts gliding across vinyl.

Ruthie, the waitress who claimed to be ninety-nine years old,

shuffled over with Marley's *avgolemono* soup and placed the hot bowl in front of one of her favorite customers. With warm fingers, she pinched the tip of Marley's nose, as if she were stealing it. And then she said what she always said: "You know, I took your father's nose the same way. . . ."

When Ruthie retreated, Teddy said, "Marisol's dedicated to those violin lessons. . . ."

"She can really play, can't she?" Wendell asked. He watched the steam rise toward Marley's sienna eyes.

Teddy exclaimed, "One day she will be in an orchestra. We can say we knew her when. . . ."

"When she didn't show up at the coffee shop," Marley added, holding back her hair so she could blow on her soup.

~

Marley was dragging. After waiting up to see Tabakov Damrosch Park, her night's sleep had felt like a nap rather a long, cozy stretch under the covers.

And yet she had been in a dead slumber, oblivious to went on around her. Sometime before dawn, for ins her mother snuck in and taped a note to the handle luggage.

"Be smart," it read. "Love, your proud mom."

There was a P.S.

"Downloaded Prokofiev's *Sonata for Two Violins.* what Tabakovic was playing—but with one violin miss so sad!"

At the end was a smiley face with the smile turned

83

Marley took the note and slipped it in her bottom desk drawer where she kept all her notes from her mom. When this was over, and Marisol's good name was restored, she would look into Tabakovic's history. Her mom was suggesting his troubled behavior came from heartache. Maybe so. Maybe he had lost a wife or good friend with whom he played duets on the violin. . . .

From the hook on the back of her closet, Marley retrieved her Time Traveler towel—the hard-to-get blue-and-orange one with a forlorn Mike Barnett stuck inside the Unisphere—and stepped into the hallway, bare feet slapping the hardwood floor. She had to get going: It was now almost three full days since the Habishaw was stolen, and two since Marisol was accused of taking it. A lot of time had passed and, to her mind, not much had been accomplished toward clearing her friend and finding the rarest American-made violin.

"Hey Dad I'm taking a shower," she sang-shouted

Oh, I need to brush my teeth, she thought. *Yuck.*

Just as she reached for the knob to the bathroom door, she stopped, seized by a sudden thought.

She remembered that when she walked along Fifth Avenue with Bassekou on the day they met, passing his "friend" Mahjoob, he knew what Tabakovic was playing.

What did he say . . . ?

Tchaikovsky. That's it. Tchaikovsky. The finale of the *Concerto in D Major.*

In Mali, do they listen to Tchaikovsky? Or violin concertos?

By the time Marley was dressed for school, pink bowling shirt with the name Lloyd in script on the breast, she knew how she would approach Bassekou.

Down in the kitchen, she shared a slice of her peach with Skeeter, who was seated in her high chair wearing only a diaper and one green sock. WNYC clattered from the radio on the fridge top.

She tapped out a phone number as she washed down her vitamin with raspberry-flavored water.

"Where are you?" she said quickly, her words almost colliding.

"Waiting for Wendell," Teddy replied, "on Columbus. Hear the traffic?"

"Have you told Bassekou about Marisol?" she asked, just as fast.

"Other than to say hi, I haven't spoken to Bassekou since last Friday night," he replied. "You know, when we were kicked out. . . ."

She told Teddy she'd call later.

Zeke Z shuffled into the kitchen, wrapped in his ratty bathrobe, his hair a worse mess than usual. As Marley squeezed by, hurrying sideways, she looked down and noticed he was only wearing one green sock too.

"Solidarity," he explained, stifling a yawn. "Whatever Skeeter's for, I'm for."

She stopped and looked up at him.

Then she took off.

"Want to get to school before Marisol bye."

"Do well," he said as she continued her flight down the corridor.

As the door slammed, he added, "Return intact."

From the moment she saw her in homeroom, Marley was assured—reassured, actually—that Marisol was totally innocent. The look on her face was a combination of embarrassment and stubborn pride: embarrassment because she knew there would be people at Beacon who would think of her as a thief, pride because she knew she was not. She had returned to school to declare her innocence and retain her rightful place among some of the city's best, brightest students.

"I can feel it," she told Marley as they walked over to sunny Amsterdam Avenue after lunch. "In the cafeteria, they were looking at me."

That's right, Marley thought. *They were.* "Marisol, they don't know what to think," she said. "But no one's down on you. I'm not hearing that."

Marisol looked up at her friend. "What *have* you heard?"

"The tape we watched from Juilliard? Ben Rosenberg gave it to me. The guys in Film are with us."

Marisol nodded solemnly.

"We're not alone, Marisol."

She hoped those words would make the afternoon a little less painful for her friend.

The rest of the school day came and went without incident. Even Mr. Noonan's algebra class. He called on Marisol early in the session, his voice and manner as blah as usual. When she answered, correctly, he moved on. Marley thought, *That's cool. He just told the class Marisol is one of us. Cool indeed.*

After the final bell, with a pretty good plan well rehearsed in her head, Marley walked from the Beacon School directly to the Sissoko apartment on East 69th, calling Teddy to tell him where she was headed. Since the Kingston Cowboys didn't meet at the coffee shop on Friday afternoons, her time was more or less her own.

The Kingston Cowboys; is there such a group anymore? Though it looked like Marisol had succeeded in her talk with Wendell's uncle, the band hadn't yet discussed when it would resume practice—or even if they would continue together. How did such a good idea, such a fun thing, go so wrong so fast?

The half-hour stroll to the East Side brought her along the south ridge of Central Park and past a queue of horses and their hansom carriages. The horses, whose tails swooshed aimlessly, ignored the sound of Marley's luggage that, bloated with textbooks for weekend study, rattled behind her on the six-sided cobblestones. As she walked along, she read from her notebook.

Looking up, Marley shook her head in dismay when she

came upon the Plaza, once a very cool old hotel that had changed a lot when they turned half of it into condominiums. Marley stopped as she remembered when her father brought her to the hotel's Oak Room for her eighth birthday. The maitre d' welcomed her as if she were the most important person ever, and then, at the table, her father handed her a gift he'd wrapped himself—a copy of *Eloise*, by Kay Thompson and Hilary Knight. Then he reached into his backpack and brought out a wrapped gift for himself—F. Scott Fitzgerald's *The Great Gatsby*. Turned out both books had scenes at the Plaza—in fact, six-year-old Eloise lived at the Plaza. Lifting his iced tea, Marley's dad offered a toast. "To the coolest people in the world," he said, a big smile on his face. "Readers!" Then they sat at their table for two and read, and soon Marley felt like she was a character in a story.

Now, turning north on Fifth, Marley put her notebook behind her back.

"Okay," she said aloud, as she nudged through a crowd of German-speaking tourists. "Let's see if I've got it."

(Like most New Yorkers, Marley wasn't self-conscious about talking to herself as she walked the streets. It wasn't unusual to see lots of people doing it. Singing too. Opera. Really loud.)

"The Republic of Mali was formed in 1960," she recited.

"The capital of Mali is Bamako.

"Bamako is on the Niger River.

"Mali is the size of California and Texas combined."

Wow, Marley thought. *That's pretty huge.*

"The population is ten and a half million, more or less.

"It has lots of natural resources, like gold, uranium, and salt and limestone and—

"Wait. Am I really going to be talking to Bassekou about natural resources in Mali?"

That last line brought a laugh from the passing tourists.

Marley blushed.

But only a little.

Marley," Bassekou said, "what a surprise. Please, come in."

He wasn't wearing a suit and tie, but instead had on something Marley had read about: a long top, very loose with wide sleeves which, in this case, were pale gold, and matching wide ankle-length trousers, both made of a kind of light-weight cotton from Mali.

Marley entered full of wonder. Seeing Bassekou dressed in native garb momentarily confused her. So did the grand piano that took up much of the living room.

She heard the door close behind her.

"I hope I'm not disturbing you," she managed, as Bassekou rolled her book bag to a closet off the front door.

"No, not at all." He gestured toward a sleek, European-style sofa across from the piano. "I was practicing, and I would enjoy a break."

"You play?"

"The piano?" He smiled. "Not very well, I'm afraid."

"Join the club," she joked.

Bassekou searched his mind for a way to compliment Marley on the way she played her electric guitar. But nothing came to him. And he would not allow himself to lie to a friend.

She pointed to the sheet music resting on the piano's stand. "Bach," Marley said, as she sat, the black leather sofa breathing aloud as she settled in. "Gavotte in G major."

"The man is spinning in his grave," Bassekou replied. "But my father insisted. Just as my teacher in Paris insisted."

Marley looked around the room. She could imagine this furniture had been bought in Paris. It was exactly like the cool stuff in the magazines her mom brought home from her business travels in Europe.

"When did you live in Paris?"

"For much of the past three years," he said as he sat next to her. "My father was assigned to our consulate on the rue du Cherche Midi."

"You speak French?"

He nodded. "Many of us in my country do."

"Because Mali was a French colony. . . ."

"I would say it's because our fathers speak it," he replied, "but yes, I suppose that is the answer, ultimately."

"You can help Marisol with her homework. She's taking French."

Bassekou said, "I could. But tell me, how is she?"

"Not great," Marley replied.

"I have heard a rumor," he said, "but I don't believe it."

A rumor?

"Someone who loves her own instrument, as she does, would not jeopardize another," he added.

"Who told you?" Marley asked directly.

"Wendell."

Not Mahjoob.

"Please tell her I am thinking of her."

Bassekou clapped his hands together as he stood. "May I show you something?"

"Sure," Marley replied.

He led her across the apartment's parquet floor toward a narrow corridor that passed a small kitchen where a woman in a long blue African-style dress cleaned vegetables in a colander, fresh water splashing into the sink. She hummed contentedly as she did her work and nodded politely as Bassekou and his friend walked by.

"Mrs. Sanogho," he explained softly. "My father's cook."

At the end of the corridor, there were two bedrooms. On the right, a master bedroom, one that was pretty formal to Marley's eyes. Bassekou's room was opposite it.

His single bed rested against a white wall decorated with an array of musical instruments that Marley guessed were from Mali. Leaning against the chair at his desk, which was across from his bed, was a contraption that looked a little bit like a harp growing out of an old, hollowed-out gourd of some kind.

"It's a kora," Bassekou said. "Would you like to hear it?"

Marley nodded. She noticed the wall above Bassekou's orderly desk was blank.

Bassekou sat in the chair and put the kora in his lap with the strings facing him and his fingers wrapped around its thin neck. He began to pick at the taut strings and soon Marley was engulfed by a sound unlike anything she had ever heard—like rainfall and twinkling stars, but maybe also like a banjo she'd heard on some old blues album.

"I don't want to bore you . . . ," Bassekou said.

"No, no. It's great. Really."

"Frankly, this is my instrument."

Marley noticed that Mrs. Sanogho had come to the door, a dish towel in her hands.

The magical dancing rainfall continued as Bassekou plucked the strings with his thumbs.

When the music stopped and Mrs. Sanogho departed, Bassekou said, "How will I ever convince my father I wish to live the life of a griot, not an ambassador?"

"A griot?"

He explained. "A griot is a wandering musician, a poet. Someone who speaks of our traditions." As he eased the kora against his desk, he added, "Perhaps someone like Woody Guthrie might be considered an American version of a griot. Or your blues singers. Taj Mahal is one, I would suggest."

"And your father says no?"

Bassekou stood. "I haven't asked. Not directly."

Marley pointed to the wall covered with African instruments. "That's a pretty big hint, Bassekou."

"Indeed." He nodded toward the blank wall above his desk. "I thought, perhaps, if I showed him our music is compatible with the Western tradition here in America . . ."

Bassekou let the thought wither.

Then he said, "That is why I intend to put on that wall a collection of American instruments. Only American instruments."

"Only American instruments," Marley repeated.

"Yes."

Just as he said to Mahjoob in the museum's gallery.

Marley shook her head.

"Not a good idea?" Bassekou asked. "I have my own savings."

"Your idea? It's great," she replied. "As for mine . . ."

chapter 9

Teddy was waiting outside the Sissokos' apartment building, happy in his '90s Orlando Magic jersey, black T-shirt and
baggy sky-blue shorts.

"Ted . . . ," Marley complained.

"My afternoon was free," he shrugged. The jersey and the
shorts were way too long: Both covered his dimply knees.

Marley walked on. "And you just happened to be on the opposite side of the park from your home . . . Standing outside
Bassekou's house."

"In fact, yes." He stopped. When Marley turned, he said,
"Not really. No. I was thinking you would go to see Mahjoob
next"—Teddy pointed sort of north, sort of west toward the
Met—"and that you would like some company."

She walked slowly until Teddy skittered next to her, passing her clanking book bag.

"No Mahjoob?"

"Bassekou doesn't want stolen American instruments," she explained. "He's starting a collection to impress his dad."

"Why would his dad be interest—"

"Because Bassekou doesn't want to be an ambassador or in the Foreign Service or whatever," she said, frustration in her voice. "He wants to be a musician. He's very serious. He knows African music, American music, blues, and Bach, Tchaikovsky. . . ."

Teddy frowned. "I didn't mean to upset you," he said, his words a tender apology.

"Oh, Teddy, I'm not upset with you." Now Marley stopped in the middle of the sidewalk. New Yorkers hurrying their way home from work parted to pass around them, never missing a stride.

"I'm ashamed of myself," she said. "I really suspected him and I had no reason to."

They waited for a wheezing bus to pass and, when the light changed, they crossed Madison Avenue, watching for turning taxis.

"Did you suspect him?" Marley asked.

Though he wanted to comfort her, he said, "No. I never did."

"Never?"

"Mahjoob, yes. But not Bassekou. Mahjoob steals."

Marley's father had said pretty much the same thing. "I

warned Bassekou," Marley said, recalling how she told him she saw them together in the museum.

"Still," Teddy said, "Mahjoob may try to sell Bassekou instruments that were stolen."

"If he does, Bassekou will tell me," she said sharply, "and I'll tell Sgt. Sampson."

Teddy was smiling.

"What?" she asked.

"You are exasperated. It's very funny."

Marley pretended to pout. She rustled her big mop of black hair. "Yeah. Basically, I know nothing."

"Except Tabakovic still uses his old instrument, and Bassekou isn't interested in stolen goods," Teddy said agreeably.

"And Marisol was an unwitting agent in the theft of the Habishaw violin. Which the police still don't have."

They turned west on sunny 59th Street. Up ahead on Fifth Avenue, crowds gathered around the beautiful fountain Joseph Pulitzer had contributed to the city a century ago. As usual, a gazillion pigeons flitted about, sparkly, gray and bold.

A new idea took root in Marley's head. "Someone made her do it . . . ," she said thoughtfully.

"Well, isn't that how somebody becomes an unwitting agent?"

"And who do we know who says he has mystical powers?" Marley asked. "The kind that might trick people."

Teddy thought for a moment. "Mahjoob."

Marley nodded. "Mahjoob."

This time they both stopped and stared at each other.

They entered in a rush, bolting past the mirror, raincoats and slickers and Skeeter's folded-up stroller.

"Dad, I spoke to Bassekou and he's buying instruments," she said as she bounded toward the kitchen.

Trailing, Teddy slowed down to sniff the air. Mr. Zimmerman, he noticed, wasn't cooking.

"We're thinking maybe Mahjoob somehow—"

Skidding to a stop, Marley all but flew out of her flip-flops.

Sitting with her father at the kitchen island was Miss Otto, the vice principal. And Sgt. Sampson, who seemed as big, sour and impatient as he had two days earlier.

"Everything is fine, Marley," Miss Otto said, as she stepped down from the stool. "Sgt. Sampson has some information he shared with me, and I thought you two should talk."

Marley looked at the brawny policeman. His scowl and dark suit were in contrast to Miss Otto's warm smile, periwinkle blouse and beige slacks.

Marley's dad said, "Some iced tea while Sgt. Sampson plays the new video."

New video? Marley thought as she squeezed past the policeman.

Miss Otto tapped the stool.

As she sat, Marley said, "Hey, Skeets."

Her baby sister looked up from her playpen and lifted one of her see-through alphabet blocks. Marley couldn't help notice it was the letter Z.

"All right . . . ," Sgt. Sampson said, as he pressed ➜ for play and then stepped aside to let the other people watch the monitor.

"That's the loading dock for Avery Fisher Hall," Marley said as the security video began. "On 65th Street, across from Juilliard."

Black-and-white midday traffic headed east in an uneven flow. A taxi passed, then another, followed several seconds later by a little bread delivery truck. Next, a man on a bicycle sped by, a plastic bag full of take-out jiggling in his wire basket.

Then Marisol hurried into view.

"Your friend," Sgt. Sampson said dryly.

"And she's still carrying the violin wrong," Marley replied.

Teddy agreed.

Suddenly, Marisol stopped rushing and stood completely still in the wash of bright sunlight.

"She looks like a zombie," Marley added.

To her surprise, Sgt. Sampson said, "Yes. Yes, she does."

Iced-tea pitcher in hand, Zeke Z said to the policeman, "You don't think she's responsible, do you?"

Sgt. Sampson replied, "I think your daughter is on to something."

On the monitor, Marisol continued to stand perfectly still.

"Not a care in the world," Miss Otto said. "Would anyone guess she was holding a priceless violin?"

On the video, Marisol looked down, turned slowly and began walking west, the violin pressed string side against her ribs and belt. Soon, she left the frame, going beyond the area covered by the security camera.

"Strange . . . ," Marley said. "She looked to the right and then started walking left. Usually if somebody calls you, you look at them, not away from them. Then you start walking."

Teddy scratched his head. Actually, Marisol looked *down* to her right side and then started west.

"On Tuesday, did Miss Poveda give any indication anything was wrong when she came to the coffee shop?" Sgt. Sampson asked.

Marley and Teddy answered at the same time. "She didn't—"

They stopped and looked at each other.

Marley continued, "She didn't come to the coffee shop. She has violin lessons on Tuesdays after school."

Sgt. Sampson said, "She didn't go to her violin lesson on Tuesday."

"Yes, she did." The diary she sent last night said so.

"Marley, I'm sorry," said Sgt. Sampson with surprising sympathy. "Her teacher says no."

Marley sank.

"Marley . . . ," her father said softly, filling the silence.

"Does she know she didn't go to her lesson?" she asked.

"No," Sgt. Sampson replied. "She believes she went."

Standing tall again, Marley said, "So that's when it happened. . . ."

Teddy looked up at his friend.

"That's when she became an unwitting agent," she said. "That's when he tricked her."

Sgt. Sampson and Zeke Z exchanged a curious glance.

"Who?" the policeman asked.

"Tell Sgt. Sampson what you've been up to," Miss Otto requested.

Marley looked at her father, and then she said, "We have a friend at Collegiate named Bassekou Sissoko and . . ." She ended by telling the policeman of her conversation with Teddy only moments ago as they crossed to the West Side.

"Mahjoob." Sgt. Sampson sighed. "Mahjoob's name is Edward Randolph Crum. He was born in Plattsburgh, New York, and as far as we know, he's never been outside of the United States. *Anywhere* outside the United States, never mind Iraq or Mesopotamia or wherever he says he's from."

Teddy said, "Really?"

"Maybe people think his act is cute, but I see him as a petty thief," said Zeke Z as he brought down glasses from the cabinet above the sink. "If he introduces Mr. Sissoko to people, it's likely they'll be thieves too."

Showing a little flash of her famous temper, Miss Otto said, "He'll try to hurt your friend."

Teddy said, "So maybe he's involved with the people who stole the Habishaw."

Miss Otto replied, "I think the key word was 'petty.'"

"Oh. Right," Teddy said. "What would he have to do with a priceless violin?"

Marley slumped again, her spirits on a rollercoaster. "Mahjoob doesn't know how to put a spell on Marisol. . . ."

"No," said Sgt. Sampson, "he doesn't."

Marley turned in the stool to look at Miss Otto and Teddy. "Where are we? We haven't done anything, and we've got to get that violin back."

"Yes," said Sgt. Sampson, "and right now, the only person who may know where it is—"

"Marisol," Marley said.

"—doesn't remember a thing."

"So," Marley said, "you believe her. You believe she didn't just rush in and steal the Habishaw."

Sgt. Sampson didn't reply.

"Yes," Marley added, a faint touch of pride in her voice. "You believe her."

As he began to fill glasses with iced tea, Zeke Z said, "Now what?"

"To cover the bases," Sgt. Sampson said, "I'll go talk to Mahjoob. Or I should say Eddie Crum."

Teddy wanted to ask if he could tag along. So did Zeke Z.

"Marley," the policeman said, "don't tell Marisol about missing her violin lesson. Our forensic psychiatrist tells us it's dangerous to interfere with a false memory."

"She might forget what really happened," Zeke Z said.

Sgt. Sampson nodded.

"I've got an idea," Marley said. "Miss Otto, do you have some time this evening?"

"At some point, I have to help my father. But, yes, I'm free," she replied.

"That's perfect," Marley said. "Antonio's would be a good place to do it." She held up a finger. "Just let me gather my thoughts. Sergeant, I can call you, or e-mail. . . ."

The policeman nodded. He would take help from any quarter to get back the Habishaw.

Teddy said, "What about me?"

"You can hang with me and Skeets," Mr. Z said cheerfully. "I'm making *cerkez tavugu*. It's a Turkish dish. A cold chicken salad with onions, walnuts, and paprika. Fresh parsley . . ."

Teddy groaned. In Turkey, it was probably very delicious. . . .

"You can come with us, Ted," Marley said as she slid off the stool. "Dad, we're eating out."

As he collected his DVD, Sgt. Sampson wondered if it'd be okay to ask the Time Traveler's creator for an autograph.

Maybe he'd get one for his son too.

Mr. Noonan was the last to arrive, and by then it was obvious Miss Otto's little office near her father's busy kitchen couldn't contain the team Marley had assembled: In addition to Mr. Noonan, who seemed surprisingly spry in his sky-blue Oxford, khakis and boating shoes, Marley, Teddy and Miss Otto were joined by Marisol and her mother, who rushed over from the little storefront boutique where she worked, terribly worried but eager to help. She clasped her hands nervously on the lap of her long skirt, which was the color of a sunflower and ringed at the hem in ruby red that matched her cotton blouse and soft shoes.

Marisol, coincidentally, wore the same clothes she had on the security videos Sgt. Sampson had presented. Marley noted that her friend still seemed exhausted, as she had throughout the school day. The ordeal continued to weigh heavily on her mind.

"Pop," Miss Otto protested now. "This isn't necessary."

"Not necessary!" he sang, with typical melodramatic flair. "My friend Marley is conducting an investigation. We cannot have six good people standing around a desk."

Marley understood the vice principal's point: Though it was a busy Friday night, her father had placed them at a prime space in his small dining room—the only table for six. This meant six customers would either have to wait outside or they'd just go off to another Italian restaurant. There were only about a million of them in New York City, and about half were on the Upper West Side.

To be honest, Marley knew Mr. Otto would do this if his daughter's office couldn't hold the team. She didn't want to take advantage of his generosity, but she needed help from smart, well-meaning people who could look at things from different points of view. She'd try to make it a short meeting.

"Vivi!" Antonio said, as he tugged the bottom of his chef's jacket. "You come with me."

Five minutes later, the Ottos returned with two platters of Italian delicacies: mint frittatas that looked like slices of quiche;

yellow peppers stuffed with anchovies and pine nuts; an octopus-and-potato salad; fried zucchini sprinkled with pecorino cheese; and more.

A tantalizing aroma rose to greet them.

"For our good neighbors!" Mr. Otto said, as he began to withdraw. "*Tutti mangia!* Everybody eat!"

"My father . . . ," Miss Otto said, shaking her head.

"My word, Viv!" Mr. Noonan exclaimed. "Don't you even think of apologizing for this."

Marisol smiled uncomfortably. She couldn't believe Mr. Noonan was showing such enthusiasm. *I guess,* she thought, *you just never know about teachers. . . .*

"I think," Marley began, "we all agree that Marisol is not a thief."

"An unwitting agent," Teddy said. He was seated at Marley's right elbow at the round table.

"Meaning somebody made her do it," Marley continued. "Against her will."

She waited until her algebra teacher finished a bruschetta made with fava-bean paste and flat-leaf parsley. "Mr. Noonan, we know you were interviewed by the NYPD and the FBI. Correct?"

"And the insurance company. They all told me they're questioning dealers to see if there's been any noise about the Habishaw. So far, no one has tried to sell it."

"But don't these dealers work with legitimate buyers?" Miss Otto asked. "How would they know—?"

"Oh, they know," he said. "It's their job to know what's

coming on the market, whether legally or not. It's a fairly small community."

"They would buy something from a thief?" Mrs. Poveda asked.

Marley noticed she had only taken a few thin breadsticks.

"They might, but at great risk," Mr. Noonan replied. "That dealer's reputation would be ruined if he were caught. The NYPD is being very aggressive."

"After talking to the curator at the Met, I have the impression we'd be in worse shape if this *wasn't* a professional job," Marley said. "You know, if she just grabbed it and turned it over to a plain old thief."

"Could be," Mr. Noonan said. "Fifty years ago, a thief sold a Stradivarius to a violinist for only one hundred dollars. The violinist kept it out of public view for almost five decades."

"One hundred dollars?" Miss Otto asked.

Mr. Noonan nodded. "Typically, they sell for one and a half million dollars or so."

"Well, this scheme is too elaborate for that kind of blockhead," Teddy said.

"The point is that the Stradivarius was missing for nearly fifty years," Mr. Noonan said.

"At least it wasn't destroyed," Marley said.

Marisol moaned.

"If this is a well-organized plot conceived by a professional who wants to profit from the theft of the Habishaw, we'll be fine," Mr. Noonan said. "The police are looking over the shoulders of dealers who might be involved in that kind of scheme. They can intervene when a deal is struck. But if it's some weirdo who likes to steal things for who knows what bizarre reason . . ."

"Going back to Marley's earlier point," Miss Otto said. "Since we agree someone made Marisol take the violin, I think the question we have to ask is: who? Whether he's a professional thief or not."

Marisol sighed in relief, pleased that Miss Otto, whom she had come to respect, believed she wasn't a criminal.

"Or why, if it was not for the money?" Mrs. Poveda added.

"Who and why," Mr. Noonan repeated. He lifted a paper-thin slice of prosciutto from the serving platter and placed it on his plate.

Marley edged her elbows onto the table. She nodded toward Mr. Noonan, who kept chewing as he put down his fork to reach beneath the table for his bag.

"Sgt. Sampson told us you remember nothing, Marisol," Marley said while they waited.

"I don't even remember not remembering," she replied.

Teddy frowned in confusion.

"But I know what I did on Tuesday," Marisol continued. "From the moment I woke up until the moment I went to sleep."

"Even at 4:46?" Marley asked. That, according to the security videos, was the precise time the Habishaw was stolen.

"At 4:46, I was going from my violin lesson to the greengrocer," she replied. "I told Sgt. Sampson . . ."

"We know you did," Miss Otto said gently, casting an eye across the table toward Marley.

Mr. Noonan passed a small manila envelope to Marisol. Her mother watched as she opened it

Carefully, she slid onto the table the photos of the Habishaw violin that Mr. Noonan had taken at the Fiske Museum and Juilliard.

Marisol studied the six photos, one at a time, spending almost a half minute with each. Then she looked at each one again, this time passing them one by one to her mother.

A waiter who had brought a bread basket to a table at the front of the restaurant stopped briefly to peer at the pictures too. So did Mr. Otto when he walked by with a bottle of red wine.

Her voice flat with resignation, Marisol said, "I know this is the Habishaw. I saw it online. It's beautiful. Magnificent. And the bloodstain . . . But I don't remember touching it."

"Can you imagine it in your hands, Marisol?" Marley asked. "If you close your eyes . . ."

They all watched as Marisol closed her eyes. But rather than put her hands down near her belt when she held the Habishaw after taking it from the display case, she held them high, as if she were about to play it—violin in her left hand and nestled under her chin, bow in her right.

Her mother's bottom lip trembled.

"No," she said, shaking her head. "I just can't remember."

Marley said, "Maybe it doesn't matter if you played it. . . ."

"It does if the man who made her take it wanted to hear her play it," said Miss Otto.

"I hope you don't take this the wrong way, Marisol," Mr.

Noonan said, "but as promising a musician as you may be, there are many violinists in New York more suited to an instrument of the Habishaw's heritage. The police are considering the possibility that one would consort with a black marketer just to play it. I don't agree, but . . ."

Marley said, "Well, that brings us to another question: Why Marisol?"

Mrs. Poveda said, "You mean why did this man . . . ?" She turned to her daughter and whispered, "*Recluta.*" When Marisol gave her the word in English, she continued. "Why did this man recruit my daughter?"

"Exactly," Marley said.

"Oh," Teddy groaned. "Now there're three things we don't know." He counted on his fingers. "One: Who took the blood-stained violin? Two: Why did he take it? And three: Why did he involve Marisol Poveda?"

Marley looked beyond Marisol and her mother to the front of the restaurant. Even though it wasn't yet seven o'clock, every table was filled. A crowd was waiting outside too, tempted by the scent of fresh seafood, garden-grown herbs and vegetables sautéed lightly with garlic.

Standing, she thanked Miss Otto and Mr. Noonan, who nodded as he continued to sample the scrumptious items on the platters. "I think we can continue this some other place," she said.

Miss Otto stood too. "You've had enough, Ira, I hope."

Mr. Noonan said, "Well, if you're offering . . ."

With a simple flick of her wrist, she summoned a waitress who began to help her clear the table.

As the three students led Mrs. Poveda out of the restaurant, Marley heard a voice.

Antonio Otto's, of course.

"Marley, wait."

In his hand was a plastic bag, the kind used for take-out food.

"You were going to leave without saying good-bye?"

"You seemed awfully busy, Mr. Otto."

His voice booming, he said, "Marley Zimmerman, I am never too busy for you!" He thrust his index finger toward the sky.

Marley and Teddy trailed the Povedas along Columbus Avenue. Their meeting would continue at their apartment, minus Miss Otto and Mr. Noonan.

"What's in the bag?" Teddy asked. "Did you look?"

"Don't have to. It's *stracciatella*. Italian egg-drop soup. It's fantastic."

"Incredible," he said, shaking his head, his mop of black hair reflecting the evening sun.

"What's incredible," Marley replied, "is every minute we spend coming up with more questions than answers—"

"—is another minute closer to when the Habishaw might be gone forever," Teddy said.

"Gone forever," Marley repeated, "and Marisol will be blamed."

chapter 10

It's frustrating," Marley said as they sat on the floor in Marisol's room, her parents at the door. "I mean, what is the motivation? That's what I can't figure. . . . The thief can't sell it—at least, not for a ton of money. The police are watching the dealers and collectors who'd want it."

"So it's not a commodity," Teddy noted.

Mrs. Poveda translated for her husband. In turn, he whispered something to her in Spanish.

"My husband says it could be a commodity one day," she said. "It has great value."

"Yes, exactly," Marley replied. "But is this kind of thief patient? Can he wait years, maybe, to sell it? I wonder. . . ."

Marisol said, "Maybe it is someone who wanted to damage the reputation of Juilliard."

"That's a good suggestion," Teddy said. "I bet Sgt. Sampson is looking into that. And Juilliard's security, too."

"On the other hand, anyone who loves—no, is obsessed with—the violin would want to have it," Marisol said. "The Habishaw is very special."

"But not everyone who fits in that category is a thief," Marley said.

"So a violin lover who is a thief," Teddy nodded. "Who also knows Marisol."

"And who can undo the top of a display case and make smoke billow into Juilliard's lobby," Marley added. "And trick Marisol into stealing the Habishaw."

Marley turned to Marisol. "Do you know anyone who fits that description?" she asked.

"No. Of course not," Marisol replied. "How could there be such a person?"

Teddy agreed. "It does sound like one of your father's characters," he said to Marley. "Maybe we should go back to the idea that what was stolen was five hundred thousand dollars sitting in the cube."

"Yes," Marley nodded, "and to the question Mrs. Poveda asked in the restaurant: Why did he involve Marisol, and not just any ol' unwitting agent?"

"Perhaps because I could care for it?" Marisol suggested.

"Marisol," Teddy said, "you were kind of rough with it."

Marley jumped to her feet. "That's key," she said, pointing at Teddy. "Whoever told Marisol to steal it didn't tell her to take care of it."

As if encouraged, Mrs. Poveda said, "Yes. True."

"So it's not someone who loves the violin," Teddy said.

"Scratch that off our list," Marley said. "We're talking about a thief who can get into Juilliard, open a display case and make smoke appear. And trick Marisol."

Mrs. Poveda looked at her husband, who was struggling to follow the conversation.

Marisol said, "*Papá, Marley dijo que es la persona—*"

Before she could finish translating, Marisol's cell phone let out a distinctive ring.

"Miss Otto," she said as she scrambled to her feet. The phone was on her belt, ready to be grabbed by her right hand, like a gunfighter in a cowboy movie.

"I told you," Teddy whispered to Marley. "She knows who it is by the ring tone."

They all did their best to avoid eavesdropping on Marisol's conversation. Of course, they all heard every word she said. "Yes. . . . Yes. . . . Thank you. . . . I will. . . . Yes." Taking a quick look at the phone, she added, "Yes. I have it now. . . . Yes. Good night."

When she snapped the phone back on her belt, she said, "Miss Otto. I can call her for help, if I have to." She turned to her parents. "You are always welcome at Antonio's."

Her parents nodded in gratitude.

Turning to Marley and Teddy, she said, "*Violin Concerto No. 23*. By Giovanni Viotti. It's a way to help me remember composers."

"And Viotti and Miss Otto are both Italian," Marley said. "A memory aid. Interesting. . . ."

*T*hree hours later, Marley was back in her room. Down the hall, Skeeter was snug in her crib, plump stuffed animals with goofy-bright smiles watching over her. Their parents were out to dinner, enjoying their Friday night date. As Marley's father once said, "Your mother is so busy, and travels so often, that I have to book time on her calendar." Marley didn't mind sitting for Skeeter. It made her feel like she'd earned her allowance.

In order to think hard and clear, Marley decided to block out all of her usual fun distractions. So she ignored the TV in the living room, and turned off the monitor on her computer so she couldn't see if new e-mails and IMs had arrived. Facebook and MySpace would have to wait until tomorrow, and so would her crazy-quilt CD collection, which now included blues by Taj Mahal she downloaded and the Prokofiev piece her mother burned for her.

So Marley was surrounded mostly by quiet. She heard only the air-conditioning that hummed low throughout the house and, every now and then, a car whooshing by. If there was any kind of event or celebration over in Central Park—and there usually was in the warm weather—she couldn't tell.

Now, as stripes of light from the flickering lamp outside the Zimmermans' brownstone spread across her rug, Marley sat on her bed and tickled the silence by strumming her guitar, forming chords without thinking about them.

A thief who can open a display case and make smoke appear. And trick Marisol, she thought. But no new images appeared, and time passed unproductively. Which annoyed her: None of the Zimmermans liked to waste time.

She wriggled off her bed and returned her guitar to its stand over in the corner where it was guarded by a framed poster of Mike Bartlett and a clunky robot from the 1939 World's Fair. On the way back, she retrieved Marisol's diary from her desk.

Where were you? Marley thought. *You were supposed to be at your lesson before you took the Habishaw. Where did you go instead?*

She looked at the paper:

```
Leave for Riverside Dr. for violin lessons
55 w/ Mr. Gabor
Food shopping
Home at 5:45, as usual—confirmed by my dad
```

You left school at 3:15, and you were at Juilliard at 4:46, Marley continued. Where were you for an hour and a half?

Interrupting the silence in her room, Marley said, "I have no idea."

Flummoxed, she thought. *That's the word.*

"I'm totally flummoxed."

She dropped Marisol's diary sheet on her desk and padded down the hall to see Skeeter. Tiptoeing into the room, she found her sister on her side, purring like a contented kitten, her hands folded together under her cheek. The sweet moon nightlight their mother had bought on a trip to Tanzania cast a gold glow onto the crib. The stars on the mobile Marley and her father had made with aluminum from soda cans reflected on the ceiling.

"Man," Marley whispered, "Skeets even smiles in her sleep."

The thought revived her drooping spirits a bit, and as she returned to her room, she decided to think about what she had achieved, and not so much about what she hadn't.

The important thing was that Sgt. Sampson and Miss Otto believed in Marisol. And the man behind the theft had become a little bit clearer, at least to her mind.

But the Habishaw was still missing.

As she watched a small boat glide along the gray-green Hudson, its sails striped in yellows and pinks, Marley felt the warm rays of the Saturday morning sun on her shoulders, revealed beneath the spaghetti straps of her bright-green top. A gentle breeze rustled her hair and stroked her cheeks. *Hot and cool at the same time,* Marley thought. *I like it.*

She turned. Ferenc Gabor's studio was on the ground floor of what looked like a castle, its big, thick stones the color of old copper. From the west side of the drive at the edge of Riverside Park, it looked like it was built long ago to protect the island from invaders from New Jersey. She wouldn't have been surprised to learn there was a cannon on the roof.

But it sure is beautiful, Marley thought as she looked both ways to cross the drive. When she looked right, she saw a statue of Eleanor Roosevelt, her hand on her chin in a thoughtful pose. Looking left, there was the crown of Grant's Tomb way off in the distance.

A breathless young boy with mousse in his hair and a white dress shirt buttoned all the way to the collar answered Mr. Gabor's inside door, but remained behind the cast-iron gate, which was covered in chicken wire. Marley figured he was about five years old, maybe six. The violin in his left hand was as big as his head.

Marley noted he was holding it properly, not with the strings against his ribs and belt.

"Mr. Gabor, please."

Before he could answer, a very tall man with flowing blond hair and pale blue eyes came up behind him and put his long fingers on the boy's shoulders.

"Thank you, Felix," he said patiently. "I'll take over."

A few seconds later, Marley heard from somewhere inside the house the sound of a bow raking across strings. She thought it sounded like a lonely cat crying, and though she didn't mean to, she grimaced.

"Ah, yes. Well . . . ," said the tall man, more or less apologizing. "In ten years, who can tell?"

"Mr. Gabor?" Marley said.

"I am he." His blue silk shirt matched his eyes.

Marley thought she smelled lavender. "My name is Marley Zimmerman. If you have a moment, I'd like to talk to you about my friend Marisol Poveda."

"Oh, Marisol," he said with a warm smile. "How is she? Better, one would hope."

Marley wasn't sure how to reply. "She's fine," she said tentatively.

"Must've been the twenty-four-hour flu." Mr. Gabor scrunched his face. "Her father said she had all sorts of distress. How gross."

"The flu . . . ?"

"Incidentally, I don't believe for a moment this folderol about the Habishaw violin. Marisol Poveda? Ridiculous. I told the police as much."

"Do you know the Habishaw?"

"Not personally. But, yes, I've heard of it. My heavens, it's gorgeous."

"It could be lost forever," Marley said.

"Yes, it could. Like all the others. We treat our instruments with care, my dear, because they simply cannot last."

Marley frowned.

"Wood and strings. A violin is but wood and strings."

"And beauty," Marley added.

As Felix continued to saw and squeal, Mr. Gabor said, "Now, if there's nothing else . . ."

"You're sure he said the flu?"

"Absolutely. When a student misses a lesson? My dear, I am forlorn. Absolutely forlorn."

He winked.

Then, his voice suddenly raspy, his words New York coarse, he said, "Look, she missed a lesson and she owes me. That's the deal. Tell her no check, no more lessons. End of story."

Then his lofty manner returned. "Good day, my dear Marley Zimmerman. Be well."

Mr. Gabor shut his door.

Marley stood still, her mouth open, arms draped at her sides, the castle walls climbing high above her.

$\mathcal{T}$he flu?

Marley slumped back across Riverside Drive, found the nearest bench and sat, her hands under the legs of her baggy white carpenter's jeans, her flip-flops rocking as if she were a child on a swing.

Marisol didn't have the flu.

Why did she lie to Mr. Gabor?

A lie makes it seem like she needed an excuse so she could be free in the late afternoon of the day the Habishaw was stolen.

Or maybe Mr. Gabor lied.

Falling into her own thoughts, Marley was oblivious to the sweaty joggers, determined little kids on wobbly bicycles with their hopeful parents trotting behind them, spry dogs dragging along their owners. She didn't even notice the small young woman who smiled a greeting and sat next to her, the *New York Times* on her lap, cold-sweating Starbuck's frappuccino in her hand. Big huge sunglasses covered half her face, her Life is Good cap pulled down low.

Had Marley looked, she would've seen the woman was a famous actress. She starred in a sitcom that was on TV in reruns at least four times a night. The characters lived right here in New York City.

The flu?

Obviously so not true.

But, if Mr. Gabor is telling the truth, why would Mr. Poveda call and say his daughter was sick? Would Mr. Poveda . . . ?

Mr. Poveda.

Mr. Poveda, who hardly speaks English.

Could he call to say she had the flu? That she had "all sorts of distress"?

No, Mrs. Poveda would make that phone call. Or Marisol, no matter how ill.

So either Mr. Gabor was lying . . .

Or another man called him and said he was Marisol's father.

A man who speaks English.

"Excuse me?"

Marley heard a voice. When she turned, she saw her reflection in the actress's elephant-ears-sized sunglasses.

The famous actress said, "Who doesn't speak English?"

Marley thought she seemed familiar. But she was too excited to try to figure out why. "Marisol's father."

"Oh." She sipped the cold drink.

"I mean, he has a little English," Marley continued, "but he can't say 'all sorts of distress.' That's an odd figure of speech, right?"

"Right." She returned to her *Times*.

Marley stood. "See ya," she said with a little salute-wave.

"Bye," the actress replied.

ℳom, I can't meet you. Going to see Marisol. I've got an idea. Call if you want. Bye."

Up early, Marley's mom had gone down to her Wall Street office for a few hours, and had invited her to a quiet Saturday lunch at the World Financial Center and then to shop for clothes at Century 21 over on Cortlandt Street. Althea Zimmerman had one minor complaint about her daughter: Marley had the same fashion sense as her father, and Zeke dressed himself with no thought at all of what to wear: stripes with checks, checks with stripes; and he mixed colors that hardly spoke to each other. He had jeans older than Marley, and his faded and ragged rock T-shirts were original issue, some a quarter-century old!

Marley hurried east, the sun rising high over Central Park flooding the side street with brilliant light, its rays ricocheting off car hoods and windshields. She crossed West End Avenue— since Hand went to bubble-headed Man just as she arrived, there was no reason yet to zigzag on her way uptown and over to Columbus—and pressed on toward Broadway, which was crowded with morning shoppers, some in a groggy-eyed search for bagels and breakfast.

At Broadway, she stopped at the curb to peer around a UPS truck that had double-parked near a row of cars at the meters. On the island in the center of the big, wide street—"It is a *broad way*," Teddy once observed—a couple in their eighties sat on a bench. At their feet were maybe a hundred pigeons bobbing at the seeds and bread crumbs raining down on them. When the jaunty, wrinkly man put a few seeds on the brim of his old brown fedora, he suddenly found himself wearing a pigeon hat. He stood carefully then did a little jig—the pigeons on his head and at his feet didn't stop their cooing and pecking—and his wife laughed in delight. Taxicabs slowed down to watch.

Marley wasn't thinking about pigeons. Her mind was trying to catalog the adult males who knew Marisol took lessons on Tuesday afternoons with Ferenc Gabor. One of them was the man who made Marisol the unwitting agent in the theft of the bloodstained violin.

Marley was sure of it.

The thief had made a big mistake.

He didn't know Marisol's dad was still learning English, and that he spoke with an accent.

Mahjoob?

Mahjoob somehow tricked Marisol into believing she had attended her lesson. That was an essential part of his scam— Marisol not realizing she had been coerced into taking the Habishaw.

But no, it wasn't Mahjoob. Or Crum, as he was born.

Crum didn't have any mystical powers. He was a creepy petty thief.

Besides, Sgt. Sampson had spoken to him, or said he was going to.

Marley thought, *Maybe I should go to the 20th Precinct and tell Sgt. Sampson what Mr. Gabor said.* The precinct house was on 82nd Street, not far from where she was right—

"Marley."

She didn't immediately turn.

"Marley!"

Wendell Justice was walking toward her.

Actually, he was trying to run, but his shins kept bumping into the laundry cart he was pushing.

"Hey, Wendell."

He wore the same white shirt as Mr. Gabor's Felix, though his top button was open and the tails flapped free. She noticed Wendell's khaki shorts had been pressed.

She looked into the cart. "Laundry, huh?"

"My mom has us checking out every place in the neighborhood for the best prices," he said sheepishly. "I tried to convince her that it's a cabal of some sort, but I don't think she believes me."

"Price fixing in the laundry business," Marley said with a shrug. "It's a fact."

In the cart, a plump hamper filled with freshly laundered clothes was topped with a smaller, rectangular brown-paper package.

"You get your school shirts laundered?" Marley asked. That could be expensive.

"No, no," he said. "Those are my uncle's—to go with his

uniform. My mom does my shirts." Suddenly, his cheeks flushed red. "Actually, the laundry cleans them and then my mom presses them."

Marley was thinking of Marisol, Mr. Gabor, Sgt. Sampson . . . "You know, Wendell, they sell washer-dryers that fit in a closet."

"We don't have a closet," he said. "Not an extra one. It's a pretty tiny apartment."

Wendell seemed embarrassed, and Marley suddenly realized she had been insensitive. She felt bad for her friend.

Apologizing, she realized, would only make it worse.

Marisol would have to wait a few minutes, and Sgt. Sampson too.

But only a few . . .

"Mind if I walk with you?" she said. "I'm going uptown . . ."

"Great," he said. "I just have to stop at my uncle's building."

He tapped the brown-paper wrapping.

"No prob," she replied. "Tell me about how you learned to play the drums. You're pretty good, you know."

Wendell nudged the wire cart onto its back wheels, and he and Marley continued north on Broadway, his heart fluttering nervously inside his chest.

Maybe Marley would like to share a couple of slices of pizza.

Or Chinese egg-drop soup.

chapter 11

Outside the stately apartment building on West End Avenue where he worked, Nicholas Justice struggled as he hauled two huge pieces of matching luggage toward a waiting taxicab. His fists gripped their handles, and he wheezed and grunted as if each bag held cinderblocks. His uniform hat teeter-tottered above his red face.

As he hoisted the bags into the taxi's trunk, he seemed to be getting a lecture from a young, radish-shaped man in a pink Izod shirt. The man pointed toward downtown, snap-jabbing his finger.

The doorman adjusted the luggage until it fit snug in the trunk, then flexed his crumpled fingers as he stood upright. Radish man continued to hassle him.

"Uh-oh," Wendell said, slowing his pace.

A too-thin woman who appeared to be the man's wife tapped her wristwatch impatiently as she waited at the taxi's backseat.

Mr. Justice squeezed past the barking man to open the yellow door.

"I bet it's nothing more than the taxi is facing the wrong way," Wendell whispered.

Marley thought, *So what? Just make a U-turn.* Looking at the man in the pink shirt, she said, "What a creep."

The woman slipped inside the taxi, her silk slacks slithering across the broad seat, and Mr. Justice closed the back door. As the taxi pulled away—and made a U-turn—Mr. Justice removed his burgundy hat and wiped his forehead with his handkerchief. Walking toward the shadows under the building's awning, he looked up and spotted his nephew and his friend.

Marley expected he'd be embarrassed—the man in the pink shirt had clearly bullied Mr. Justice because he knew the doorman couldn't really argue in return. If he did, he might lose his job.

But Mr. Justice suddenly brightened, and the tension vanished from his face as they approached.

"Wendell, is this your good friend Marley Zimmerman?" he asked with a broad grin. "Marley Zimmerman? Daughter of the famous 3Z. And of Althea Fontenot Zimmerman, senior vice president at—?"

"Yes," Marley said. "That's me."

He thrust out his hand.

She really didn't want to shake it—she knew he was playing her, acting like a grown-up version of the 3Z scruffs who'd hang outside her family's brownstone—but she did.

"Sorry I didn't recognize you, Marley," he said, as he adjusted his burgundy jacket. "It's been one heckuva day. Say, you go to Beacon, don't you?"

"Yes, sir. I do."

"Your friend Marisol, she's in some kind of trouble, isn't she?"

"Uncle Nick," Wendell said as he steadied the laundry cart. "She didn't do it."

"No, I'm sure she didn't," he replied. "Seems like a fine young lady—"

"Hey, Wendell," Marley said suddenly. "I've got to run."

"Oh. You sure?"

She patted him on the back. "People, places . . . You know."

"You tell your parents Nicholas Justice said hi," Wendell's uncle exclaimed. "Would you do that?"

She nodded.

Backing away, edging uptown, she looked at Wendell.

She said, "Later."

Wendell's face turned beet red. Tomato red. Cherry red. Something like that.

Marley was still miffed at Mr. Justice's insincerity when she arrived at the busy 20th Precinct. A harried cop at the desk told her Sgt. Sampson was out. Marley thanked her, left her cell phone number and marched out, putting the sergeant's card back in her pocket when she returned to 82nd Street.

Standing amid the white-and-blue NYPD patrol cars parked like check marks at the curb, she looked east, then west, all the while considering what she'd do next. It was too late to take the subway downtown to have a mellow date with her mom.

She speed-dialed Marisol.

Voice mail, the greeting in two languages.

"Marisol, it's me. Call right away. Bye."

She double-checked her cell. No, she didn't have Marisol's home phone number.

Maybe she'd walk over to the building where her father was one of the supers. No, his shift had ended. He had either just gotten to sleep or was out with his family.

Go to the boutique where Mrs. Poveda's employed? It wasn't far from here. No. No sense in upsetting her—working among all those colorful clothes, great fragrances, and inquisitive customers probably gave her a chance to think about something other than what had happened.

What next?

"Teddy, I know you're with your sister and cousin, but give me a call. Bye."

She needed to figure out who pretended to be Marisol's father when he called Mr. Gabor.

That man was *involved*.

That man took Marisol out of her routine.

Turned her into a zombie who didn't remember she'd missed her lesson.

That man who had her under his control when the Habishaw was taken.

Who could it be?

"What's up?"

Marley's father was absolutely drenched in sweat. Which is what happens when you jog five miles around the Central Park Reservoir in sneakers, cut-off denim shorts, and a sleeveless flannel shirt. With Skeeter up front in a stroller.

Skeeter in her little canvas hammock, bouncing, jiggling, laughing. In her Time Traveler bucket hat, Hawkgirl T-shirt and diaper.

"I'm thinking," Marley replied. "Hard."

She was on a stool at the kitchen island, blowing on her spoon, sipping the *stracciatella* Mr. Otto had given her and she'd reheated when she returned home from the Two-Oh.

"It's, like, 142 degrees out and you're having soup?" he asked.

Poor Skeeter. Resting in his sweaty, bony arms. Not that she minded. She tossed off her hat and kept giggling.

"Almost as dumb as jogging at noon when it's 142 degrees," Marley replied.

"Ouch," he said. "I have been put down."

"I'm sorry," she said quickly. "My mind is, like, really, really throbbing."

"Unwitting agents and all that?"

"Liars and thieves and somebody who would trap a sweet kid like Marisol."

He walked gingerly around the island and placed Skeeter in her playpen. "Okay if I shower first?"

She shrugged. "I don't know if you can help, Dad. It's a big mess, and I'm nowhere."

He ventured back toward the sink to wash his hands. Over the rush of water, he said, "I'm really sorry, Marley."

"I know."

Carrying a damp facecloth, he returned to Skeeter, who had already started organizing her blocks.

"You've done a lot, Marley," he said. "The police believe you, and your vice principal does too. I'm sure Marisol would be in a lot more trouble if it wasn't for you."

Skeeter scrunched, squinted and smiled as her dad wiped her hands and cheeks.

"Yes, but meanwhile, no Habishaw."

Through the steam rising from the bowl, Marley looked over at her father as he tended to her baby sister. His hair was a wild curly mop, all knotty and chaotic as usual. Despite the air-conditioning, he still dripped sweat.

She noticed a bald spot brewing at the back of his head, and she knew his ankles hurt when he ran.

"I love you, Dad," Marley said. "I'm sorry I snapped at you."

He stood. "I know." He tapped the center of his chest and then pointed at her with the same long finger.

She did the same. It was their signal.

He drop-plopped the cold cloth onto Skeeter's head. "Cucumber cool, Skeets."

Marley watched her sister wrestle it down and resume cleaning her own face.

"Egg-drop soup, huh? You know," he said, "I've been thinking of trying my hand at making that. I got a recipe from Papua New Guinea. . . ."

As he pounded upstairs, Marley decided she'd bathe Skeeter in the sink when her father's shower ended. That always lifted her spirits. Skeeter's too.

"By the way," he yelled from above, "the four of us are having dinner tonight. Together!"

That warmed her heart as much as the soup did.

I am never going to be able to concentrate completely on Marisol and her make-believe father and Mr. Gabor and the Habishaw until I wipe that insincere man off my mind. Nicholas Justice.

And with that thought, Marley marched up to her room. Her cell phone at her elbow, the computer speakers blasting Beck's *Guero*—a good cross-generational compromise choice in the Zimmerman household—she googled Nicholas Justice.

Lots of Nicholas Justices: Sixty-two hits, in fact, and just one had to do with Wendell's uncle.

According to the *New York Times'* website, four years ago

a man named Nicholas Justice was accused of involvement in a scandal at Lincoln Center's Rose Hall. Mr. Justice and another security officer would sneak people through a side entrance into jazz concerts—for a fee they kept for themselves. The *Times* said the two men were fired from their jobs.

Justice wasn't just a judgmental phony. He was a thief. He didn't just quit to get a better job as a doorman. Lincoln Center told him to go away.

She couldn't find any other articles on that scandal, and a search under "N. Justice" returned more than 37,000 hits.

"Doorman" and "upper west side" returned too many hits, too.

I'm getting farther from it, she thought, as Beck's chinga-chinga guitar played off the beats.

What else do I know about him that makes him different from all the other Nicholas Justices?

Well . . . His father was a carnival barker.

"Okay," she said, "let's make it 'Justice' and 'carnival barker.'"

A second or so later, she muttered, *"Holy . . ."*

Marley sat back in her chair.

More than a thousand hits—1,213, to be exact.

First on the long list was a site dedicated to Jedediah Justice's Traveling Amusements.

Which was managed by the Jedediah Justice's Traveling Amusements Historical Society.

Marley scanned the site.

Justice's Traveling Amusements.

Operated as far south as North Carolina.

As far north as New Hampshire.

From 1960 to the year Marley was born.

April through Labor Day—and beyond!

The largest, grandest, funnest—funnest?—traveling amusement park and midway in the whole U.S. of A.

Featuring a roller coaster, Ferris wheel, carousel, mechanical bull and Kiddoland.

Pony rides. A petting zoo.

Bobo the Elephant.

Carnival games of skill and chance. (Win prizes!)

Caramel apples, ice cream, and cotton candy.

A fireworks display each and every night.

And our special attraction—Mesmero, America's Legendary Master of the Ancient Art of Mesmerization!

Mesmerization. "What is . . . ?"

She leaned forward and turned down the music's volume.

Then she clicked on the name Mesmero and was sent to a special page dedicated to him.

Wow, Mesmero looked like Dracula, only in white tie and tails. His arms at shoulders level, fingers outstretched as if he were shooting invisible rays at someone.

Mesmero.

She went to Wikipedia.

Nothing on Mesmero, but soon she had made her way to a site about somebody named Franz Mesmer.

Okay. Here we are. Animal magnetism. Also known as mesmerism.

"'The evolution of Mesmer's ideas and practices led James Braid to develop hypnosis in 1842.'"

Hypnosis!

She click-jumped to the section on Braid.

"Bang," Marley said as she read carefully, thoroughly. She bounced in her seat, hopping to fold a leg under her. "Bang!"

Braid led her to the American Psychological Association's definition of hypnosis.

She read aloud. "'When using hypnosis, one person is guided by another to respond to suggestions for changes in subjective experience, alterations in perception, sensation, emotion, thought or behavior.'"

"Like making a good, honest person steal something," she said, as if talking to the computer monitor. "That sure is a change in behavior."

She backtracked to the Justice Amusement Historical Society's site.

No reference to Nicholas Justice or his brother, who was Wendell's late father.

But she found a photo of Jedediah Justice.

Wow. He looked like a grown-up version of Wendell.

But he wasn't Mesmero.

Marley stood. Paced.

Stopped. Folded her arms.

Closed her eyes.

Just like she told Marisol:

Close your eyes and think.

"Mmmm . . ."

She imagined a couple of kids running around a big ol' carnival. In a huge field in the middle of somewhere. Or in a stadium parking lot outside a big city.

A gigantic party every day from noon until the fireworks blasted off at midnight. Loads and loads of people celebrating, little kids giddy—it's like Disneyland had come to their neighborhood!

But no party for those workers.

They had to toil sweaty-hard to set up the carnival and then harder to keep it going for a steamy week or two. Hustling for hours and hours and hours every single day for five long months.

(When Marley concentrated real, real hard, she could smell what she saw and hear real actual sounds. Now she saw and heard sledgehammers driving posts in the dry, dusty earth to tie huge colorful tents to, and she smelled the grease on the tracks of the rollercoaster and under the Tilt-a-Whirl cars.)

Then those carnival workers had to pack up a bunch of trucks and cars, go traveling in the dead of night and move to a new city and another state, doing everything all over again.

And again and again and again, throughout the broiling hot summer.

Through all that, who are those two Justice kids going to play with?

Who are they going to want to be around?

Who can entertain and amuse them?

Their father, who has to be in charge of everything?

The grunting, sweating, busy workers?

Bobo the Elephant?

No.

Mesmero.

With his deep, piercing eyes and X-ray fingers.

And maybe Mesmero taught them how to hypnotize people, just for the heck of it. To amuse them, and himself.

And maybe Nicholas Justice remembered how to do it all these years later.

Marley opened her eyes and stared at the computer screen. Her screen saver was up.

She was on a bench in Central Park. Teddy on her left, Marisol on her right. Big smiles. Cheese!

She said, "But when could Mr. Justice have hypnotized you, Marisol?

"Not when we were at band practice.

"Not when we were leav—"

Suddenly, Marley felt a jolt way deep down in her body.

"When you went to see him! By yourself!"

Excited—maybe more excited than she'd ever been in her life—she ran to her door, flung it open, and screamed, "Dad!"

Startled, Mr. Zimmerman, who was downstairs in his office, shouted, "Marley. Are you okay?"

"Dad,getuphererightaway.I'vegotit.Iknowwhathappened.Dad, hurry!"

Even before her father reached the top step, jumping two at a time, Skeeter on his hip, Marley was shouting into her phone.

"Teddy.Teddy,whereareyou?I'vegotit.Mesmero.Hypnosis.Call me now."

With her father peering over her shoulder, Marley read everything she could find on mesmerization and hypnosis. By the time she finished, she was certain she was right.

chapter 12

Marley ran all the way from her family's brownstone to 93rd Street and Columbus Avenue—a distance of almost a mile— her flip-flops slapping the hot concrete and soggy asphalt as she zagged around yipping dogs, delivery boys on bikes and slow-moving shoppers. She arrived panting and parched, and was now as sweat-soaked as her father had been.

Forgive me, she thought as she stepped into the little vestibule of the Povedas' apartment building. *I hate to wake you up after you worked all night, Mr. Poveda, but . . .*

As she was about to press the bell, she turned to see Mr. Poveda and his two sons.

"Hey, Marley," said Boli.

"Hey, Marley," said Cristian.

"Hello," said Mr. Poveda.

Marley saw his tentative smile.

"Mr. Poveda . . ." She was out of breath. *"¿Usted sabe donde está Marisol?"*

His eyebrow raised, he replied, *"Ah, no sabía que usted también habló español, Marley."*

"I don't." Gasp. "A few lessons . . ." She took a deep, deep breath. "Marisol. *Donde . . .*"

"Marley?"

She turned. Marisol was standing behind her, in her hand the rings of a plastic shopping bag filled with husky ears of corn.

Marley said, "Where have you been? I called." No time for air kisses now.

Putting down the bag, Marisol ran her hand along her belt to find her cell phone. "It's off," she said as she lifted it. "We took the boys to the Pied Piper Children's Theatre."

Her breath beginning to return, she blurted, "Marisol, I have to talk to you. I have news."

Mr. Poveda excused himself, tapping Boli and Cristian on the back of their Mets caps to shoo them inside. He nodded his good-bye to Marley and his daughter.

"What?" Marisol asked, tugging the front of her pink blouse over her midriff.

"Tell me about your visit to Wendell's uncle on Monday afternoon. After you left the diner."

"I already did. Marley, what's going on?"

"Tell me again. In detail. Marisol, please."

Marisol shrugged. "I told him that we were good kids. That we were serious students—"

"Yes, yes. But can you remember anything unusual happening?" *Before* he hypnotized you, she wanted to add.

"No," she said, shaking her head. "I spoke to him and he apologized. Then the lobby was very quiet, and he asked me if I would like to—

Marisol's cell phone interrupted, beckoning her with a strange, tinny ring tone.

Exasperated, Marley grimaced at the annoying noise—until she realized what the song was. Then her eyes opened wide.

It was that odd, insistent piece of oompah music that's played at circuses and carnivals and even at the Central Park Carousel when the wooden horses go up, down, and around.

"Marisol—"

Marisol quickly snapped off the phone, ending the irritating sound.

Then, as she returned the phone to her belt, she stepped forward, bumped a shoulder into Marley, and proceeded to walk south along the avenue.

The bag of corn collapsed on the sidewalk.

"Marisol?"

Marley's friend kept walking, her head held high, her back rigid.

"Marisol . . . ?"

Marley trotted to catch up.

Marisol's blank expression was exactly the same as it was in the security videos.

Like a zombie's.

"Marisol, wait."

Marley stepped in front of her friend. She reached out and put her hands on her shoulders.

Marisol's eyes were empty orbits, her pupils dilated.

"Marisol . . . ? Say something."

But Marisol didn't reply. She edged around her friend again, squeezed past a parking meter and walked to the corner. She looked both ways, then crossed Columbus and continued south.

"Marisol . . ." Her voice trailed off.

She could *not* believe this was happening in bright sunlight on a beautiful summer afternoon in New York City.

"Wait!"

Marisol walked on, unyielding and without emotion.

With nothing else to do—or at least nothing that came to mind—Marley followed her.

A half mile or so later, never separated by more than twenty feet, the two friends crossed Broadway and began down the slope toward West End Avenue.

And then they walked along the north side of the wonderful old building where Nicholas Justice was employed as a doorman.

Steam was coming out of Teddy's ears.

Not literally, of course. But he was furious. *I'm not a baby,* he thought. *I'm me, I'm happy to be me, and I'm proud of me.*

And more to the point: *I don't want to dress like the men in Soho. I would look ridiculous in aviator sunglasses, a sharp-cut Italian wool blazer, fitted silk shirt, tightly tailored jeans and pointy-toed boots.*

What kind of thirteen-year-old wants to look like a model posing in Milan or Paris or New York City?

I can't even grow stubble on my face!

"Look around. Do you see anyone who dresses like you?" said his sister Kiana, as she pointed a long manicured fingernail toward the busy, buzzing boutiques that lined sunny West Broadway. She was as tall and lean as her brother was short and stout, and her hair shimmered down her back.

"Nobody like me here, no," Teddy replied wryly. He clutched rectangular shopping bags in each fist. The bags were filled with blouses, light sweaters, camisoles and T-shirts Kiana and their cousin Mei bought, one item costing ridiculously more than the next.

"What do people think when they see you?" Kiana asked, as they slalomed through shoppers and milling tourists.

"Yes, what do they think?" Mei added. "Tell us."

Kiana said, "Your image is the *most* important th— Oh, Mei, look!"

She lifted up her sunglasses, grabbed Mei by the elbow and veered quickly toward another crowded shop. This one sold shoes.

Teddy found an uncomfortable bench in the corner of the store.

"Conspiracy," he groaned as he began to dig through the shopping bags to find his cell phone.

*H*er back against limestone, Marley waited on the side street as Marisol entered through the revolving doors.

She was certain Justice had mesmerized Marisol and compelled her—that was the word: *compelled*—to take the Habishaw. The carnival music was the trigger to activate the suggestion he had planted in her mind: "When you hear it, come to me." Hypnotists did it all the time on TV—getting people to cluck like chickens or do crazy dances on a word or sound command, and the audience would laugh hysterically.

But there was nothing funny about this. Marisol was in danger.

Marley edged carefully around the corner and stole a quick glance inside the building, expecting to see Marisol with Nicholas Justice, all phony and snarky, with Marisol under his control.

Taking out her cell phone, she prepared to dial the Two-Oh and ask for Sgt. Sampson. She'd let Justice hear the call. Even if the policeman was still out, it would have an impact.

With her thumb, she tapped the 212 area code.

Then, darting through the shadows, she burst boldly through the revolving doors.

Justice was not at his station. The vast lobby was empty.

And the steel door that led to the basement where the Kingston Cowboys had held their very brief rehearsal was closing ever so slowly.

Burying the phone in her pocket, Marley raced to grab the door before it banged shut.

It took a moment for her eyes to adapt to the darkness.

But she heard the zombie-step slap of Marisol's huaraches on the cement stairs.

She followed, and soon she was belowground.

She saw Marisol entering the wooden shed near the boiler where Wendell stored his drums. It was wide open. The padlock had been removed.

"Marisol," Marley hiss-whispered. "Wait, Marisol."

Following, peering through darkness, Marley watched as her friend nestled in a corner.

"Marisol?"

Suddenly, out of the shadows behind them, Nicholas Justice appeared.

"You!" he shouted.

Marley's heart seemed to leap in fear as he drew closer, closer.

"You helped her steal that violin!"

The blank expression on Marisol's face didn't change.

"Wait until the police get here," he said, as he leered angrily.

"Right," Marley said. "When they get here, they'll learn about you."

"Oh really?"

"That's right. You hypnotized her!"

Justice laughed. "And who will believe that?"

"You did. You are—"

Before Marley could finish her sentence, Mr. Justice raised his right palm in front of Marisol's face. Quickly, he recited, "Three, two, one" and snapped his fingers, making a sound as loud as a gunshot.

Marley watched as Marisol blinked and shook her head as if waking from a long, confusing slumber.

"Marley . . . ?" she said, as she looked around. "I . . ."

Justice reached and tugged the rumpled canvas that had been tossed over Wendell's drums. He gathered it into a roll in his arms.

On top of Wendell's drums was a white box, the kind that held dozens of long-stemmed roses.

Dropping the paint-splattered canvas, Justice pulled the string on the naked bulb above their heads. Raw bright light filled the shed, momentarily blinding Marley and Marisol.

"Open the box," he demanded. "Go on."

Marisol opened the box and began to dig through a layer of foam popcorn. Her hands trembled with fear.

She reached into the box.

And withdrew the Habishaw violin.

"Oh, Marisol," Marley said.

Slowly, she raised the Habishaw. Its bloodstain seemed to glow in the harsh light.

"Marley . . . ?" Her bottom lip quivered.

Justice stepped back quickly and slammed the door shut. "Ha! You're caught!"

Marisol looked at Marley, looked down at the Habishaw in her hand and began to cry.

"Marisol, don't," Marley said. "He hypnotized you. Don't listen to anything—"

"Do you remember that, Marisol?" he said, a sneer on his thin lips. "Do you remember my hypnotizing you?"

Marisol was confused. In fact, she had no memory of what had happened. She didn't understand why she was no longer in front of her apartment talking to Marley as her father and brothers made their way upstairs.

And she had no idea why the Habishaw was in her hand.

"Where's your witness?" Justice challenged.

"I'll tell them," Marley said, stepping toward the doorman. "They'll know it was you—"

"Do you think the police will believe you?"

"Yes," Marley shouted. "Your father was a carnival barker and you knew Mesmero and he taught you! It's a fact!"

The information she screamed was important, yes. But so was the volume: Marley wanted the first-floor residents to hear, or people passing through the lobby. Her voice rang out louder than the Kingston Cowboys had played their music, louder than Justice had shouted.

"And you know Juilliard. You were a security guard at Lincoln Center who was fired. For stealing!"

Justice's face grew harsh in fury.

"You're the one who's caught!" she shouted. "Mesmero!"

Snatching the padlock from his pocket, Justice rammed it in place and then snapped it shut.

"The police will handle you two," he said.

Marley reached between the slats and grabbed his tie, but his gray clip-on came off in her hand.

"Mesmero!" she screamed.

Their hearts thumping, Marley and Marisol stared at Justice as he stormed toward the stairs.

"Mesmero!" Marley screamed.

"Marley . . . ," Marisol whispered. She shivered in fear. "He's—"

The heavy door to the lobby banged as it closed.

"Marley, we're trapped." She stared at the floor, the Habishaw quaking in her hand.

The overhead bulb cast peculiar shadows along the shed's sides where old luggage and cardboard boxes were stacked at odd angles.

Though both teens were sweating, they found no relief in the cool air below earth.

"Marley . . ."

"Marisol, listen to me. Look at me."

She reached and grabbed her friend.

"Marisol, you didn't do anything wrong."

As if to contradict Marley, Marisol held up the Habishaw.

"Marisol, you were trying to save the Habishaw. That's why you took it."

"I don't under—"

"I read that people who are hypnotized won't do something that's against their principles. You wouldn't steal, Marisol. But you would save a beautiful violin if it was in danger from a fire. He used your character against you."

"He's going to hurt us."

"No," Marley insisted. "He won't. He can't."

"We're trapped."

"Marisol, we'll be okay," she said.

But the creepy walls of the tiny shed said otherwise. On the other side of the wooden slats, the boiler seemed a callous sentry.

"I told Teddy. He'll come," Marley said. With a smile, she added, "The buddy system. You know. . . ."

But Marisol wasn't placated. Not a bit. Here she was, locked in an overcrowded wooden shed and, despite what Marley said, all she could see was the reality that she was now holding a valuable violin she'd been videotaped stealing from a display case at Juilliard.

Her family's dreams would be destroyed, and she would go to prison, branded forever as a thief.

"Besides," Marley said, "if he calls the 20th Precinct, Sgt. Sampson will come and we'll explain everything."

Marisol slumped. "He's right," she said. "They won't believe us."

"Sgt. Sampson will find the records that show Justice was fired—"

"We are just us, and he is a man of authority and no one will believe us and not him—"

"Marisol," Marley said, "that's why they *will* believe us. Because we are just us, and you are not a thief."

Marisol shook her head.

"You are not a thief," Marley said. "Your reputation, Marisol . . . That is worth more than the word of that ugly . . . That . . ."

With nothing else to say, Marley screamed. "Mesmero!"

"Mesmero!"

That last one was so loud and so shrill, the Habishaw vibrated in Marisol's unsteady hand.

Teddy looked at his cell phone and frowned curiously. An excited message from Marley demanded a callback, but now when he tried to reach her, he went straight into her voice mail.

"Teddy. Teddy, where are you?" she'd said. "I've got it. Mesmero. Hypnosis. Call me now."

No, Marley wouldn't wait for his call, for his counsel. Marley took action, always.

He tried again. Voice mail.

Concerned, he stood and, keeping an eye on the shopping bags, tried Marisol's number.

Voice mail, too.

Something was wrong. He felt it in his soul.

He waved his pudgy arms overhead until Kiana turned, staring angrily at him across the congested sales floor.

Then he waved good-bye and ran out of the store.

$\mathcal{B}$y now, the salty sweat on Marley's skin had dried, and her desire for a drink of water had turned to need.

Teddy, she thought, *where are you?*

"No one is coming," Marisol said. She'd stopped crying, but she kept shifting in the small space, the Habishaw cradled like an infant in her arms. "It's been an hour. More than one hour."

According to the clock in Marley's phone, it had been fifteen minutes.

But it had felt like an hour.

"Too bad we can't get a signal down here," Marley said as she stared at her cell.

Soon the silence was disturbed only by the rush of water through the tangle of overhead pipes. The familiar, comforting sounds of the New York City streets were long gone.

"Nobody's coming," Marisol said.

"Yes," Marley replied, "they are."

A moment later, Marisol added, "Mr. Justice will lie."

"Of course," Marley said. "He has to."

$\mathcal{T}$eddy had a thought, and just before rushing down into the station to take the C train uptown, he made one last call.

But there was no answer at the Zimmerman residence.

Her voice soft as a child's, Marisol said, "Are you worried?"

She had noticed that Marley had stopped shouting. And that she had gone on her tiptoes to tap on the water pipes with the side of her cell phone.

Marisol nestled the Habishaw against her little body as if she were protecting it from harm.

Next Marley ripped masking tape from the lids of countless boxes, finding old books and photo albums and bills and receipts and various other yellowing documents. Clothes too: baby pajamas and tiny T-shirts. Booties and blankets.

Maybe we'll find silverware, Marley thought, as they brought down another box from a shelf. *A knife, maybe.*

But they found nothing to use to pry open the big lock on the shed.

And nothing to help burst through the wood: They learned a folding chair didn't work very well as a battering ram.

But as she rummaged deep below the bottom shelf, Marley found a folded cardboard box that was empty except for an instruction booklet.

"What's this . . . ?"

Across the booklet's face were the words HIGH OUTPUT SMOKE GENERATOR.

The smoke in Juilliard's lobby . . .

"There was no fire," Marley muttered. "Whoever spoke to the *Times* didn't have the right information. . . ."

"Marley?"

"This is evidence," Marley said, holding it so Marisol could see. "And, look, it has a timer. There's probably a serial number—"

"You didn't answer me," Marisol said. "Are you worried?"

"I'm thirsty," Marley replied. *His toolbox,* she was thinking. She wanted to find the tools he used to open the display case.

"And you are sure he will not hurt us?"

Marley remained quiet. *But,* she thought, *there's no telling what a cornered rat like N Justice will do.*

chapter 13

Marley heard the upstairs door open, and saw a rush of light.

"They're right here," Justice said. "The two of them, and the violin. Unless your friends destroyed it."

They saw Justice's black shoes, the stripes of his gray slacks, the pockets of his burgundy coat, and then they saw all of him. His ferret face was bright red from heat and anger.

"Wouldn't surprise me," he continued, gesturing with his hat, his hair a sweaty mess. "I would've returned it, but they locked themselves in there with it."

Teddy was behind him.

"They stole it and now they'll demand the reward," Justice said.

"Open it, please," Teddy said.

"Not until they agree to let me return—"

"Open the shed," Teddy insisted. "Open it now or you will be in more trouble than you can imagine."

"Now listen here, young man—"

"Now!"

The stark fury in Teddy's voice startled Marley. It also made her smile.

At that moment, the upstairs door opened again.

Sgt. Sampson rushed down the stairs.

Justice suddenly seemed confused.

Marley reached her hand between the slats. She had Justice's gray clip-on in her fist.

Sgt. Sampson glowered at the doorman. "Do what he said. Open the door."

Justice lurched toward the door. As he fumbled with the lock, Marley whispered, "Mesmero."

The lock came off and the door swung open.

Stepping back, Justice said, "I can't wait to hear what lies—"

As Teddy watched, Sgt. Sampson nudged him to the side. "You all right, girls?"

Marley nodded as she walked toward him.

The Habishaw nestled in her arms, Marisol didn't budge.

"Marisol," the policeman said as he held out his hand.

"I'm afraid to move it," she replied softly. "Can I hold it until someone from Juilliard arrives?"

"Now she cares!" Justice laughed. "The thief!"

Marley joined Teddy. His face soaked in sweat and gripped with fear, he offered her a bottle of water.

Marley gobbled the cool drink to soothe her parched throat. And then she gave her brave friend a hug.

"It's all right, Ted."

"I called the police, but when I didn't see them I thought . . ."

"No, no, Ted, it's all right."

Pointing angrily, Justice said, "They're in it together."

"Sergeant," Marley said as she stepped toward the policeman. "He hypnotized her."

"Ridiculous," Justice snapped.

"Your forensic psychiatrist can show you how he used Marisol's cell phone as a trigger."

"Sergeant, are you going to listen to—?"

"Quiet!" That was Sgt. Sampson, his voice so forceful that Teddy jumped.

Marley said, "Remember when we saw Marisol on the second video? She looked down and to the right before walking off to her left toward Amsterdam?"

Sgt. Sampson nodded. Teddy did too.

"She keeps her cell phone on her belt on the right. That circusy ring tone told her to report to this building."

"And I suppose I hypnotized her into stealing the violin *by phone*?" Justice asked sarcastically.

"You didn't need the phone for that," Marley said. "Marisol came to see you on Monday afternoon, the day before the Habishaw was stolen. You two were alone, and that's when you planted the suggestion."

"Go on, Marley," Sgt. Sampson said, as he stared at the doorman.

"After she saved it from all that smoke, she ran outside and that's when you called her. She brought the Habishaw here. Where you could store it. In a locked shed," Marley said, pointing. "You have the key. We don't."

She turned toward Sgt. Sampson.

"See, he had it in that box in there. I bet his fingerprints are on the tape." She looked up at the policeman. "You'll find the box for his smoke machine too."

Another police officer squeezed through the curious tenants who had gathered on the steps.

"Him," the sergeant said, snapping his chin toward Justice. "And, Jackson, get someone over here from Juilliard to handle the violin."

"You're arresting me?" Justice protested.

"Sergeant, his cell phone. Please," Marley said. "Just in case . . ."

He nodded and held out his hand.

The doorman looked up at him. Defeated, he surrendered his phone.

Officer Jackson took Justice by the elbow.

"She's not a thief," Marley shouted as Justice was led away. "No matter what you say, she's not."

Though her voice cracked, everyone heard her.

On a bench below a bulletin board jammed with official notices and photo of the Two-Oh's softball team, Teddy entertained Skeeter, who seemed to be helping him negotiate "Pat the Bunny." A noisy fan nudged musty air around the busy room.

As Zeke Zimmerman, Cristina Poveda, and Gus Poveda waited, dozens of police officers scurried in and out of the precinct house. Several dragged in unsavory characters and quickly scuttled them out of sight, their hands cuffed behind their backs, a pitiful look of resignation on their faces.

Lawyers arrived and disappeared to where the accused criminals had been taken.

Though she was a lawyer, Marley's mother knew corporate law and criminal law were two very different things. But she represented Marley as she gave her statement. When the Povedas' lawyer couldn't be reached, she sat in with Marisol too.

As Sgt. Sampson questioned her, Marley was direct and straightforward, describing what she had learned about Jedediah Justice's Traveling Amusements and its star attraction Mesmero. She told Sgt. Sampson that what she read about hypnosis helped her understand how Justice had manipulated Marisol.

"I guess Justice saw I didn't like his style," she said, remembering her brief visit with Wendell earlier today. "Then his nephew probably mentioned that we were trying to figure out what really happened. Justice panicked. I guess maybe he thought Marisol would show up alone and he'd let you find her with the Habishaw."

During her interview, Marisol was tentative and frightened.

Mrs. Zimmerman asked for a moment, and Sgt. Sampson and Dr. Moon, the forensic psychiatrist, left the little pale-blue room.

"Marisol, *el policía sabe que usted no ha hecho nada mal*," she said, her arm draped around her shaking shoulder. "Don't be afraid."

"I don't remember."

"Fine, then. Tell them. Tell them the truth."

And when Sgt. Sampson and Dr. Moon returned, she did.

She said, "I decided to find out why Mr. Justice had judged us so harshly. We were only trying to play music together. All right, not very well, it's true, but still . . . It's a very good activity for us. But I could see that Marley and Teddy believed he didn't want us there because of who he thought we were, not because of our music. I am *not* inferior, and I wanted to know why he treated us so poorly. To confront him, yes, but also to understand.

"At first, he didn't want to speak to me. He walked away. Surely, I thought, Marley and Teddy are right. I told him I was an excellent student at a very, very good school and that my parents are outstanding people, and I don't deserve to be treated this way."

Sgt. Sampson asked, "What did he say?"

"He apologized," Marisol replied, "and he asked me not to repeat anything to Wendell or our friends." She shook her head. "I felt he was sincere. . . ."

"Did he mention the Habishaw?"

"I don't remember. But I did mention that I played the violin."

"Do you remember anything about the hypnosis?"

"Nothing," she said, "no."

"Where did you speak to him?"

"At his desk. Then by the fireplace."

"You don't remember leaving the lobby?"

Marisol said, "My memory is that we had a useful conversation. What I remember next is going home."

Sgt. Sampson nodded.

He looked at Mrs. Zimmerman. "Dr. Moon needs a few minutes. It could help her."

"I'll advise her parents," Marley's mom replied.

"Otherwise, I'm done here." Sgt. Sampson stood.

When Mrs. Zimmerman stood, Marisol did too.

The policeman towered over her.

"You're a good kid," he said, as he leaned down and rapped his knuckles on the table. "Miss Otto and Mr. Noonan are right."

"Thank you," she said. "Is the Habishaw . . . ?"

"It's fine," he nodded. "You took good care of it, Marisol."

Marisol looked at Mrs. Zimmerman and sighed in relief.

"Let's go," said Marley's mom, holding out her hand.

Marley's throat was still raw from screaming, but having Skeeter on her hip and Teddy at her side made her feel much better. So did Sgt. Sampson's report that the NYPD had searched Justice's apartment and found a set of duplicate keys from Lincoln Center he had made while he worked there in security. One of those keys gave him access to the loading dock at Juilliard. The police believed Justice snuck in late at night to tamper with the display case when it was in storage, and also set up the smoke machine and a timer.

"It looks like he was planning on stealing the Habishaw," Sgt. Sampson said when he joined the Zimmermans and Teddy at the Two-Oh. "Involving Marisol gave him some cover—a degree of separation from the actual theft."

"Do you think he always planned to hypnotize someone to do it?" Marley asked.

"Probably. But then Marisol told him she played the violin. That made her a more plausible suspect."

"Did he have a buyer lined up?"

The policeman shrugged. "Not that we know of. He might've been waiting until the heat died down. But we got him, Marley. Thanks to you . . ."

By now, the September sun had begun to set behind the Jersey Palisades, and Marley felt the lift of an autumn-like breeze as it drifted across town.

"I don't mean to pry," Teddy began, "but Wendell's uncle said something about a reward."

"The insurance company," she nodded. Moments ago, after the Povedas headed uptown on their way home, their gratitude as abundant as their tears, Marley mentioned the reward to her parents. There was instant, and silent, agreement on the matter.

"Marisol found it," Marley told Teddy as they approached 72nd Street where Amsterdam and Broadway met—about the most chaotic intersection on the Upper West Side. "She found it and took care of it."

They waited for Hand to go to Man. Marley hoisted Skeeter, securing her hold on her baby sister, who was clutching her bucket hat with two fists, as if she remembered 72nd could be one of the windiest cross-streets in Manhattan. And soon it would be, as summer surrendered to the latter part of the year.

"Without her, Justice would've done something terrible to the Habishaw," she said.

"You think?"

"He couldn't appreciate beauty like that. Marisol does."

Her parents drew up behind them.

Marley turned and smiled when she felt her father's hand on her shoulder.

They knew Wendell wouldn't come to the coffee shop on Monday—after all, he had avoided Teddy all day. He'd found a new route to school, leaving Teddy standing amid the hustling crowd on Columbus. Nor did he even glance at him in class or in the hallway. Of course, all text messages and phone calls went unreturned.

Teddy said Wendell looked terribly sad.

On Tuesday, he had no choice but to visit his new friends. Teddy and Bassekou were waiting for him outside Collegiate. They threatened to carry him by the armpits if he didn't agree to come along.

Said Bassekou, his bearing as imposing as his manner was thoughtful, "You do not want to make a scene."

Wendell protested. "I—"

"We're friends," Teddy explained.

Marley and Marisol were at their table.

Pale and fidgety, Wendell couldn't look at them as Bassekou nudged him into the booth.

"There's no trapdoor, Wendell," Marley said. "You can't escape."

Finally, he raised his head.

Marisol said, "What about the Kingston Cowboys?"

Sliding in alongside Wendell, Teddy said, "I have a proposal."

"Okay," Marley said. "What is it?"

"Well." He cleared his throat. "As a quartet, we are not good."

Bassekou shrugged and nodded at the same time.

Wendell had yet to turn to look at Marley.

Teddy said, "But as a duo, Marisol and Wendell could be quite interesting. So . . ."

"You and I practice until we catch up," Marley said.

Bassekou thought, *Oh, this means either Wendell and Marisol do not play with their friends for several years, or Marley and Teddy enter a very intense period of study.*

"Wendell?" Marisol asked.

He puffed his cheeks. Though the temperature had dropped into the mid-sixties following Sunday's downpour, he had sweat beads on his forehead and upper lip.

"I want to explain about my uncle," he began, as he clutched the table.

"Not necessary," Marley said. "That's not on you."

"But it is," he replied. "He did it for me."

Teddy was incredulous. "He stole the Habishaw for you?"

"For the money I'll need," he explained. "For Collegiate, college, graduate school . . ."

Marley leaned in.

"After my father died, my mother was worried that I'd fall in with the wrong crowd and get in trouble and stuff. The public high school wasn't too great where we used to live," he said. "That's why we moved here—for Collegiate."

Marley couldn't see Wendell as a troublemaker. But she kept listening.

"My uncle told me that, before he died, my father often said he wanted me to be something better than he was," Wendell added, his face growing red from embarrassment. "And my uncle said he didn't want me to grow up to be a doorman."

"A doorman is a respected profession," Teddy said firmly.

"This city couldn't exist without them," Marley added.

"You know what I mean," Wendell replied. "He said I should go to Collegiate, then an Ivy League school and one day I would live in the kind of building where he worked."

"There is nothing wrong with that," Bassekou said. "Though his method . . ."

"He said he was going to sell the bloodstained violin to a collector who'd take care of it, and then we'd have the money for my education."

Marley tilted her head. She wasn't buying it. Nicholas Justice didn't use Marisol to steal the Habishaw so he could help Wendell. He was a plain old thief and he ripped off Juilliard last month just like he ripped off Lincoln Center four years ago when he pocketed money from jazz heads. He was a liar and a—

"Your uncle is an idiot," Teddy said suddenly. "But you're not. Marisol, can we put this behind us?"

She nodded. She saw that Wendell was as nervous as she had been in Miss Otto's office a week ago. And much like her, he had done nothing wrong.

She said, "Let's talk about Teddy's proposal for the Kingston Cowboys. . . ."

As Marisol began discussing a strategy for the little group, Marley held out a fist.

She said, "We're cool, Wendell."

He tapped Marley's fist with his.

". . . the important thing is to keep working on the right sound for our band," Marisol continued. She looked at Bassekou. "Marley was saying she thinks a kora might be intriguing with a violin and Western percussion. . . ."

"A kora?" Wendell asked. "You mean the harp from West Africa? I love that sound. . . ."

Soon, the group fell into a long discussion about music. Wendell rattled off names of musicians from Mali, and Bassekou mentioned his favorite American musicians. When Marisol asked how the kora was tuned, Bassekou quickly rattled off his reply, momentarily confusing Teddy. But then Marisol said, "Diatonic scales in F. You know, the major is 'do, re, mi . . .' Ted, the Chinese used Bassekou's tuning about twenty-five hundred years ago."

"That's way before anybody from the West visited Asia," he replied.

"Or West Africa," Bassekou nodded.

"Or New Jersey." That was Wendell. Everyone at the table laughed.

Happiness restored, Marley looked around for Ruthie, their waitress. She was thinking now was a great time for a bowl of Greek egg-drop soup.

about the author

JIM FUSILLI is the author of five novels set in New York City, including *Marley Z and the Bloodstained Violin*, his first for young readers. His short fiction appears in many anthologies, including *The Best American Mystery Stories*. He's also written a nonfiction book about Brian Wilson and the Beach Boys' album *Pet Sounds*. Since 1983, he has written about rock and pop music for *The Wall Street Journal*. A musician and songwriter, Jim and his wife have a daughter in college.